CHAPTER 1

Glasgow. June 16th. 05:15. Gary Scott, 71, woke up and pulled himself out of bed, drawing the curtains and having a look outside to gauge the weather. It looked pleasant enough. No rain for the moment and he could see, by the rustling in the trees, a light wind coming in from the north. Rory, his dog, was already sitting upright behind him, waiting in anticipation for a 'Aye', or 'Naw' walk decision displayed respectively through a smile, or a shake of the head. As soon as Scott turned towards him he raced to the door and pulled the chain off the door handle. 'Mind reader,' Scott laughed to himself as they left the flat. It was early in the day, but already light. 'Nice and fresh,' Scott smiled to himself taking in a lungful of the passing breeze as he and Rory stepped onto the deserted Park road. As he walked along Scott's thoughts drifted briefly to past days – the army, the girl, jail… He lived alone now, retired and single. Just his dog, his pension 'and square sausage, rolls and fish fingers' to keep me going, he smiled. 'And the Doublet bar just across the road, of course, the icing on the cake…' They walked past the pub and as always he looked at the door he had first opened as a young eighteen-year-old. He was already looking forward to his couple of late afternoon pints and of course, the banal chat, anecdotes and laughter with the regulars. They reached Eldon street. He stopped out of habit, as always, though there were hardly ever any cars at this time. The near silence was calming, there was only the sound of the wind dancing with the tree leaves and the deep hum of the M8 at Charing cross, not far off a mile away. It sounded like a river was gushing through the center of Glasgow.

…Ian Smith had been walking quickly down University Avenue, heading for Bank street, when he heard the call from behind. It was Ware- drunk and with a demented look on his face. 'Ian- I want to talk to you now-who were you texting- wait, you wee cunt.' Ware was jogging and was no more than fifty meters away. Smith was glad he had got a text off to Liz, but now he had to get away from this bastard. He would get to his hotel and tell Liz everything in the morning. Looking over his shoulder at the fast approaching Ware and getting worried, Smith started to run himself. He reached Kelvin Way and turned left. Reaching Glasgow University Union and still running he turned once more to see how far Ware was

THE DOUBLET DETECTIVE.
HIT AND RUN

DAVID R.D. ROLLO

ISBN 978-1-957582-44-3 (paperback)
ISBN 978-1-957582-45-0 (eBook)

Copyright © 2022 by David R.D. Rollo

All rights reserved. No part of this publication may be reproduced, distributed, or transmitted in any form or by any means, including photocopying, recording, or other electronic or mechanical methods without the prior written permission of the publisher.

Printed in the United States of America

WESTPOINT
PRINT AND MEDIA

For lost friends and family, my kids,
and a wee bit for myself.

behind him as he went to cross the road leading to Bank street…

Gary Scott was about to step onto the road when he heard something from up around the Union. 'A squeal of brakes a muffled bump-a small skid?' He hesitated, stopped and pulled back Rory, who had started barking and listened - cocking his ears. It had been some sort of car crash for sure, he determined. For a moment or two there was silence, then he heard a roar of a car engine and he looked up to the top of Gibson street. He saw what looked like a Mercedes take the corner at speed and head rapidly down the road. Alarmed, he instinctively tried to see the driver through the tainted windows. As the car approached the driver started to come into focus – it looked like it was a female. Then the car was passing him. It was a blue Mercedes and the driver was definitely female. Old, not young, which surprised him a little. There was a surreal moment as he caught the driver's eye. She looked terrified as they connected for a brief second and then she turned her gaze back to the road and shot past. Gary Scott stood still for a second. He looked back up toward the top of Gibson street. Nothing. He thought of going up to have a look, but the hill was a bit steep at his age and despite his curiosity, he couldn't be bothered going all the way up to possibly see nothing. It came to him half an hour later as he was throwing a stick into the Kelvin for Rory to fetch. He knew that women in the car…

but where from? It wasn't that recent, but he knew her for sure…

Eight hours later in a flat opposite where Gary Scott lived, Stuart Hislop stirred the sugar into his mug of tea in the kitchen, staring into the whirlpool effect as he did so. He was of medium height, stocky and bearded. Considered a handsome man. As he stirred, he thought. He could hear his wife Liz, moving around in the bathroom. He stopped stirring and set his gaze on the wall near the front door. He heard the bathroom door shut as Liz moved to her bedroom. Her bedroom, not theirs anymore. Scott's face tightened. He waited. Ten minutes later she appeared. Looking gorgeous, as she always did. Smooth and shiny jet black hair, tall and slender. Something seemed to move inside him. Lust and anger frothing up and racing to his brain. Again he thought, 'How could she have done that?' Liz was wearing a tight cream dress and black high heels, her breasts pushing hard against the soft dress and revealing a full cleavage. Her eyes darted around the room as if trying to remember what she had to do. She glanced at him quickly a couple of times and them immediately diverted her eyes. She had always had an air of vulnerability about her- one of the reasons Hislop had liked her so much. She hesitated a moment and then came over and kissed him. It was just a peck on the cheek, but it was perfunctory- cold. He did not react.

'Ok. I'm off. The guest should be arriving about three and I need to tidy the flat up,' she smiled, taking a quick sip of his tea. 'How much sugar did you put in this?' she pulled a face. 'Ok, got to go. I might go to the shops after…'

Stuart, following his suspicions, had looked at the Airbnb booking. It was for a guy who looked about thirty from his profile picture. One guest. From Canvey Island in England. 'Might go shopping after'. Give yourself some time… He felt the bile again. 'Who was she sleeping with, how many was she sleeping with…?' His fists clenched without him noticing. She reached the door and turned for a second. He tried to smile, but couldn't. Strangely, compared to the last few weeks she paused a little longer than normal. She appeared to be about to speak. Then she shook her head, evinced a look of disappointment and opened the door and left. He heard her heals clicking down the stairs as she descended and listened as they receded towards silence step by step. It was if she was walking out of his life forever. Not knowing how prescient his thoughts would soon prove to be, he took a sip of his tea and shook his own head. 'It can't go on like this – I have to sort this out,' he thought, admonishing himself for his continued reluctance to confront her. Once again, thoughts of revenge grabbed his mind…

CHAPTER 2

The Doublet bar two weeks later. Sam Morris sat at a table facing the bar with the door a meter or two away on his right hand side. Being a self-appointed fastidious man of control, who craved routines, ('familiarity breeds content' he often said), he always looked to sit on the same chair. Near the bar and near the door to pop out for a cigarette. Apart from when he was away on his many travels from his casino days, he had been coming to the pub for forty-four years. He had once worked out the number of pints he must have had in the Doublet and how much he had spent, realising with a shock he could have bought a wee flat with the aggregate, before quickly justifying the expense to himself as money well spent for the comfort and solidarity of warm friendships the pub had provided him. Morris ordered his second pint and a vodka for Shona, who had come in for a quick one before meeting her friend Myra for lunch and had joined him at his table. After some general chat she said. 'So that's it - you have finished with casinos Sam. Not tempted to travel away again…?

Morris shook his head firmly. 'No way- that's me finished. No more wondering cowboy stuff. I'm sixty-two, call it a day. I have my wee flat here and my son, so I'm ok. Margaret my daughter, is coming back from Greece soon too. I always missed Glasgow, funnily the older I got the more so-no- back for good.'

'You've been lucky to get abroad so much and those casino scams you told me about-amazing. You should try and write a book about them…you don't miss it- not a bit bored now? she asked.

'No, not at all. In fact, thinking about it makes me just glad I got through it all. Too many close calls with some dangerous people. No-a few pints here- see my family. I'm happy'. They chatted a little more before Shona left to get the underground to Hillhead. Morris fancied and ordered a Guinness from Morag behind the bar. He sat at the table by himself, reading the National from time to time and looking around the pub. Big John was there as he was every single day and half the night. 'Must be ten pints a day' Sam figured. 'Forget a wee flat- he could have got a three-bedroom house…' He noticed Gary Scott or Captain Birds Eye due to his well-known and often announced predilection for fish fingers, sitting at the bar, instead of the tables. He came in every evening at four twenty and left at seven, more or less on the dot. Sam had talked to him on occasion when up at the bar. Decent guy. Had been in the army in Ireland but he preferred not to talk about it too much. Moved back up to Glasgow from Newcastle a good few years ago. Had got into some trouble down there with a women- had spent some time in jail - Morris recalled. Scott didn't like to talk about this either. He always had his dog with him and was an early riser hence the early exit time from the pub. He was getting a bit old now –seventy or so. Presently, Morris went to the bar, ordered another Guinness from Gordon, said hello to Scott and then went back to his chair nodding and saying a quick hello to fellow Doubleteers. He was relieved that Phil Burns aka as 'The Philosopher' was not in. Once he pulled you into a conversation, there was no escape mentally, or physically. One or two of the regulars had asked the owner to bar him due to his insistent and annoying conversational threads, but he always replied with a wink, 'Why should I retreat him differently from the rest of youse.' Stuart Hislop was in too. Morris got along with him well. Always went out of his way to help others. Ex school teacher. His wife had left him a week or two ago Morris recalled and it showed on Stuart's face. He looked drawn and troubled. He had been besotted with her Morris remembered-it must have hurt - as it had to him all these years ago with his wife and with Linda more recently. 'Linda, Linda…' he shook his head as he thought about her. He had not seen her since their fight a year ago and he realised again with a pang that he missed her. Yet again he had the same flash back of her that dogged him regularly. Morris, suddenly wanting the diversion of company, decided to join Hislop since he was not often in and he looked like he could do with some cheering up. He picked up his Guinness and moved towards him.

'Hi Stuart,' he said, sitting on a chair opposite him. 'You alright…haven't seen you for a bit?'

'Hello Sam. How's it going? Aye, I'm ok, I suppose. Trying to stay off the booze a little. Don't want to get a reputation…' He smiled briefly and looked into his pint. Morris glanced at it too and laughed. 'A bit late for that now-you missed that boat about twenty years ago! So did I, come to think of it…' Morris got a couple of pints in and Hislop and he chatted away, soon warming to each other's company. Hislop was glad to talk to someone- Morris' presumption had been right - and soon they were laughing about old days and characters. When they finished their drinks Morris looked around.

'Bugger this ... Fancy a pub walk into town-end at the Horseshoe?

Hislop looked at him and smiled, wavering for as long as three seconds.

'Well I shouldn't…a man of moderate drinking, my impeccable reputation…Aye, what the hell. Tomorrow is another day. Just a few pints mind, none of the hard stuff. Share a taxi back?'

'Absolutely.' Morris smiled, pushed his chair back and swept his arm across his stomach. 'After you sir…'

Morris woke up the next morning and made a coffee in the kitchen. He took it back to bed and sat up against the pillow and lit a cigarette. His thoughts drifted back to his conversation with Hislop who, by the time they and got to the Horseshoe, was drunk and darting between anger, mirth and sad contemplations so rapidly that he was hard to follow. Not that Morris was that far behind him. They had reached the stage that any third party dropping in on their conversation would not have had a clue about what they were talking about. As the drinks had flowed, the conversation had gravitated towards Stuart's wife, Liz. He had been reluctant to talk about her, but bit by bit, his obvious anguish had come out. Stuart had told him that the last time he saw her was two weeks ago after she had gone out to meet a new guest at their Airbnb flat in Wilton st. That day, Stuart had phoned his pal, William Ware, but they couldn't meet in Glasgow so Stuart had taken the bus to Stirling University, where Ware worked at the University. He got too pissed to come back, so stayed the night at a local hotel. He had sent Liz a late message when he realised he wasn't going to make it back, but there had been no reply, which was not particularly unusual given their current relationship.

'I didn't get back home till about six the next day as I had a few medicinals in here...' Morris remembered him saying.

Stuart had come home and Liz had not been there. Later he looked in her bedroom and he noticed her clothes had been tidied up and some were missing. She was gone.

'A bit rude of her to just bugger off without saying anything, for Christ's sake...' Morris vaguely remembered drunkenly saying.

Stuart had just shrugged in apparent resignation. 'Aye, maybe. I'm worried but Sam. Something is wrong, I'm sure. It's been two weeks now and nothing. Not a call. Her best friend Anne Smith called asking for her –she hasn't been in contact with her either. I also phoned as many people as I could think off. Nothing- Liz hadn't contacted any of them. Remember Anne - you met her with me and Liz a couple of times?' Morris nodded as Stuart continued. 'They talked nearly every day before...Poor Anne as well- her husband Ian was killed in a hit and run accident about the same time as she buggered off. Police called a few days later asking me where Liz and I were at the time of his death- as if we would be involved! He was a good pal of mine as well. It never rains...'

'Maybe you had better call the police about Liz.' Morris had said, getting slightly worried himself. 'I'll have a word with my police pal Alisdair Frazer at the

Dumbarton road polis shop. You remember him- been in the Doublet…?'

'Aye think so, the guy from the Highlands-West coast- Ullapool?' Hislop had nodded.

'That's it. Known him from way back - good cop. Deputy Chief Constable now. Don't know if he knows exactly what to do about missing persons, but he will have some idea. I'll speak to him tomorrow - see what he says - and if he recommends it you should maybe notify the police. Did you check the Airbnb guest? Did he go to the flat you rented out?'

'Must have,' Hislop had replied, 'I looked at the bookings comments. Guest said she was a good host, had given him all the information he needed and mentioned that he had put the keys back through the letter box when he left. I collected them a couple of days after. The flat looked fine…no clues there.'

'I reckon the police will check that out anyway if they chase this up. The whole thing sounds a bit strange,' Morris had said.

'Aye, it is. We were having some problems, but to just leave like that…I don't know what's up. I just want her home and to talk it out. Should have had the balls to do it before and now look…'

Now, still lying on his bed, his coffee nearly finished and the cobwebs clearing, Morris recalled his promise to contact Frazer, had a shower and another coffee and gave him a call. Frazer was off that day, and

Morris asked if they could meet for a drink. Frazer had a shopping trip to do and would not be free till seven.

'I'll try and hold out till then,' Morris had said and they laughed down the phone.

Sunday at seven. The Doublet was quiet. Just a few hangovers in the alcove, discussing the madness and embarrassments of the Saturday night before. Few comments, but occasional forced laughter and shaking of guilty heads. Morris and Frazer arrived within a minute of each other. Morris got two pints of lager in and immediately ushered Frazer to his usual table. Frazer was dressed in smart slacks with a blue Polo shirt. He was not as tall as the stereotypical Highland cop- being only 5'10, but he was broad, fit and strong. His hard muscles honed not from the gym, but from hard craft in his youth and now maintained through running and swimming. They chatted amicably for a while about football, family, politics and then Morris related Stuart Hislop's story. Frazer listened quietly then spoke.

'You know Sam that about eight people a day actually go missing in Scotland. And more-the police get thirty or so calls a day about lost people. People get worried too easily. Their daughter is an hour late getting back from somewhere and its call the polis time. But, from what you are saying about Stuart and Liz, is it? it sounds a wee bit different. First thought I had was that she has run off with another guy. No contact with Stuart you can maybe understand if that's what happened, or they had had a fight, but if so, she would have been on the phone to this best friend you mentioned Anne all day discussing the situation. That fact makes me worried that something has happened to her, or she harmed herself. Unless she has decided for some unknown reason to make a clean break from everybody she knows, even including her best friend? Right…what to do? Firstly, I'll try to keep an eye on this personally since it's your pal. If I passed it on it would just get buried in paper work. It wouldn't be considered a priority at this moment anyway. Ok…if considering the possibility that she has been harmed in some way, initial suspects would be Stuart himself of course, the Airbnb guest -since she does not seem to have been seen since that day - and we will need to check with her family and other friends. Also need to try and find out a place she would be likely to go if she was depressed, or wanted to get away from everyone for a while. You might need to help me out Sam, in an unofficial capacity of course, with talking to people and traveling. I can oversee the whole thing and have the contacts and authority, but I can't spare the men at this time, as that hit and run up at University Avenue is still unsolved and I can't be away from the office except days off Sunday and Monday.'

Morris nodded and agreed to help in any way he could. He remembered Hislop mentioning the Hit and Run accident on their boozy excursion and the victim, Ian Smith, was a good friend of his.

He turned to Frazer. 'For the Hit and Run thing you said, I think you already know that Stuart and Liz were good friends of Ian Smith? You talked to them I'm sure- Stuart said the police called him a few days after the accident. Anne too- what did she have to say?'

Frazer nodded. 'Aye we know Ian and Anne knew the Hislops. Since we have no witnesses we made an appeal and also asked Ian's family and friends about him and their own whereabouts at the time of the accident. Anne said they had had an argument and he had left the night before. Obviously we were a wee bit suspicious. She said she was at her Newsagents at the time of the accident, saying she had gone there to pick up a bottle of wine she had left when buying cigarettes, the night before. At five twenty-five in the morning it seemed a bit strange, but we checked it out- true enough. Shop had just opened, she was the first one in, papers had just arrived, so the owner remembered the time. Ian Smith was found dead in the middle of the road at five twenty-seven by a young guy out for a jog. He was smart enough to check exactly when he found the body. Post mortem said that Smith had had died as a result of violently hitting his head on the road and it was consistent with being as a consequence of being struck with a vehicle travelling around fifty miles per hour. He had a broken leg and pelvis too.

Some blue paint on the right leg of his trousers. A postman came forward after our appeal and said he had passed the Uni at five twenty, give or take a few minutes and seen no body- so time of the accident was between five twenty and twenty-seven when the jogger found him. So Anne ruled out. She mentioned her and Iain's other close friends- your Stuart and a guy called William Ware. Called them. Ware said he has a flat in Glasgow, but was in Stirling at that time and your pal Stuart said he and Liz were at home at the time of the accident. I guess she left that day, or the next. Anne's family- a sister and brother are both down in England. Anyways, from all of these we were only slightly suspicious of Anne, but her alibi is fine. Bit odd that Liz just disappears just after, but can't see any connection at the moment. I'll keep it in mind though.'

Morris and Frazer sat for a minute in silence and sipped their pints, thinking.

'You don't think maybe Liz is dead, or something do you?' Morris asked.

Frazer replied immediately. 'Liz? Doubt it - but there is always that possibility to consider and the longer there is no contact the more likely that is, but let's see what we can dig up first.'

Despite the drink. Morris felt entirely sober when he got home. His son was out and he was about to start dinner when he thought a walk and a takeaway would be good. He phoned Kevin and he readily agreed to a Fish supper from the Philadelphia. He walked up to Great Western road in the rain and stood behind the small queue. He decided he would not tell Stuart more than that he was going to make some unofficial enquiries. After ordering two fish suppers and a single steak pie he went outside for a smoke and phoned Stuart while he waited.

'…nothing to worry about pal-just be quicker than delegating it,' he said when he got through. "He wants me to check a few things out though…' he said, trying to reassure Stuart. Morris suggested they meet for a coffee in the morning for a chat.

'That serious?' Stuart had attempted to say in a jocular tone, but it had only come out as frozen words of concern and despair.

In the morning Morris met Hislop at a Greek coffee shop on Great Western road that his son had recommended. Yiannis, the friendly owner, ushered them to a table in the corner and brought over two double Espressos. Morris explained that he had met Frazer and that he and Morris would try and help them find Liz.

'…but Stuart, I need to know everything about her and you. If things get going you will need to be checked out too, so be prepared for that. It's sort of unofficial just now, it's not actually been too long since she left, but there are some worrying signs. Just tell us all you can, even if you think it is nothing relevant. I know we talked about it a bit in the pub, but give us the full story from start to when she left…'

Stuart took his gaze from Morris' eyes, looked out the window for a few seconds and then let out a long breath.

'Ok…right. We had been going through a bad patch since something happened. This is between you and me as much as possible Sam, right…?'

Morris nodded as Hislop continued.

'…It was about two months ago. I remember the date in fact- first of May. I was supposed to meet an old school pal of mine Colin McGregor at the Shoe, but he never turned up and I came home early. I had told Liz I would be out till late evening earliest. I opened the door and heard moaning from the bedroom. The bedroom door was closed, but it was unmistakable Sam-she was shagging some bastard. I did nothing- just walked straight out and went and got hammered in the Doublet. I remember Anne Smith came in a wee while later, but I was in no mood to talk to anyone and she must have picked up on that and stayed away. She could maybe tell you the time and the state I was in though, if she remembers. She doesn't go in that often, so she might. Anyway, when I got home again, Liz was in the kitchen making dinner and acting as if nothing had happened. I was pissed, but couldn't even confront her. I just went to bed, in the spare room. The next day was the same. I couldn't face the truth, but I just couldn't bear her confirming it and giving me details. Sad bastard eh? She gave me a lot of odd looks, but never asked me what was up. She's as bad at confrontation as I am. That was basically it and that's how it continued till she left. We stopped sleeping together, but she seemed to want to tease me, wearing more and more sexy things. As I said. I had moved into the spare bedroom from the beginning and it started driving me crazy what she had done in our bed. And she just kept acting as if nothing had happened which only made me think it wasn't the first time…'

He stopped for a minute, then continued. Morris said nothing, wanting to hear the full story first, but he glanced into Stuart's eyes and saw the pain.

'I had no idea who the guy was and still don't, but the whole thing just festered inside me like burning acid. I should have left, threw her out, or at least cleared the air, but I'm a damned coward. A couple of days before she disappeared we went out for a meal with Willie and Ian and Anne. It was a thing we did every month, so I felt loathe to cancel and Liz was keen enough, especially to see Anne, despite us barely talking. What a disaster that was. Willie was constantly rude to her, Ian just sat there boozing and Anne got smashed and shouted at the waiter a couple of times. I apologized to Ali, the owner, but I could see he was pissed off. On the day I last saw her she was teasing me again - wearing sexy clothes as she went out for the Airbnb booking. I actually remember thinking that I had to speak to her that night, but instead I phoned Willie for some company. He has a Glasgow flat but he was in Stirling- he is a lecturer and was working that day. So off I went to meet him when he had finished. We got hammered big style. Mostly talked about Liz, of course. I stayed the night at Stirling Court hotel and came back in the afternoon. Needed a few pints at the Shoe to get my act together, got home at tea time and she was gone. No calls-no note-nothing. I phone Anne nearly every day to check and she calls me often too. Mostly pissed and tearful.' He started shaking his head. 'If you knew how much I miss her Sam…'

Morris realised it was his cue and spoke.

'Shite. That's a bad one alright. On your own bed. For God's sake. Aye, I know you love her, but if this continues and after what you told me, you have to realise you will be the main suspect. I'll help you just now in any way I can. Best thing I can do meantimes is to verify what you told me. I'll talk to Anne, that guy in Stirling-who was it again- William…Willie? and this Airbnb guy might have something that could help. So since that first day not a word? You think she is sulking, or –I'm sorry- maybe with that guy in the bed? Another coffee?' he asked raising his hand to get the attention of Yiannis, who took the order and came back with two single Espressos.

'I don't know what to think,' Stuart continued. 'I sort of feel, or maybe it's hope- that she is just in a mood and will come back tomorrow. But it's always the next day and it hasn't happened yet. But I tell you the minute she gets back, or even phones, I'm going to tell her about what I heard and we will see what happens.'

'Would you want her back after what happened?' Morris asked with genuine interest, thinking of his own relationship breakdowns with his wife and Linda.

'I really don't know' Stuart replied. 'I have asked myself that a thousand times. Just now I just want to know she is safe and after that we will talk and take it from there. Can you give up loving someone for one infidelity, I don't know…If she fucked off with some guy you think she would have at least said- left a note- told her best friend…something. I could almost accept that-it's the uncertainty of not knowing she is at least ok somewhere…'

They both sat for a moment their minds drifting, judging and passing sentence on their respective relationships.

CHAPTER 3

Hislop had supplied the names, addresses and numbers of the three persons Morris wanted to talk too and after a call to him, he headed towards Stirling in the afternoon to meet Professor William Ware. As he drove on the M80 he was already planning his next visit and calls. That night he would try and get hold of the Airbnb guest, Roy Shorrocks. Hislop had shown him his Airbnb profile. He lived in Canvey Island in Essex- and his phone number was included. Anne Smith lived in Partick and Morris planned to meet up with her soon too. Meanwhile, he had updated Frazer who fully agreed with his plans and reiterated that Morris update him as soon as he had contacted or met the three.

Morris passed through Stirling town, turned left at the bridge and was soon parking in Stirling University car park. It was ten minutes to four. Ware had arranged to meet him just after the hour after his last lecture for the day on Asian History. Morris found his way to the coffee shop as arranged and waited for Ware who had said he could not be mistaken for anyone else, being 6ft 7 inches tall and hair down to his shoulders. Right enough at five past four a scarecrow like figure strode into the coffee shop looking around purposively. Morris waved him over, introduced himself and thanked him for the meeting. Morris noticed he was wearing brown corduroy trousers which, apart from hanging on pegs in charity shops, he had not seen in years. Morris laughed to himself, remembering how they were once the height of fashion. That and his long hair made it look like Ware had strode into the coffee shop straight from the 70's.

It soon became apparent that Ware - as Hislop had indicated and being Hislop's oldest and best friend- was well up to date on Hislops and Liz's situation. Behind his smiling demeanor, Morris got a sense that Ware had little sympathy for Hislop for not confronting his wife for a month and a half before she had left and nothing but contempt for Liz for the pain she had caused to his best pal.

'Excuse my language, but I would have gone straight into the bedroom, kicked the shite out of the guy, thrown the bitch outside with the bed closely following behind. Then gone out and got pissed and start looking for a new, better partner, the next day…'

'Well maybe,' Morris had said a little surprised by the professor's strength of feeling and language. 'But he said he just couldn't bring himself to confront her. I can also understand that. The truth can hurt and some people want to avoid it being confirmed to them. So tell us what happened on that day he came up here. He was still tormented by what she had done?'

'You can say that again. It hurt me to see him so desolate. He had been like that since she shagged that guy whoever it was. You know him, but I have known him since he was a teenager. He had some tough family issues then, but that all seemed behind him after he met Liz. It was marvelous to see him so happy. I watched her very closely too when we all met up. I'm sure she loved him as much as he did her. They were genuinely happy. Only problem was that she could not have kids, but they accepted that early on. You can ask anyone. Stuart came alive when he was with her. He used to just look at her when she was not looking and smile. Somehow she would pick it up, turn to him and smile back. The whole damn thing is a tragedy. What the fuck did she do that for? Let's hope she turns up and maybe they can work it all out between them. I'd never take her back though, I could never forgive her for what she did to Stuart - but maybe Stuart would… no news on where she might be at all?'

Morris shook his head. Ware confirmed that Hislop had stayed the night at the nearby Stirling Court hotel on the night before Liz had disappeared. The Police could check that out easily enough if he recommended it, but he was not seeing Stuart as a potential murderer at this stage anyway. They chatted generally a bit more and then Ware excused himself as he had a tutorial at five, got up and stride out the coffee shop.

Morris thought carefully on the drive back to Glasgow. Ware was not the quiet, erudite, Professor type he realised he had anticipated him to be before the meeting. His language, too, seemed incongruous with his academic status. Morris could not help but feel it was a bit of an act. Ware was steadfast in his opinions, both about his friend and Liz. That seemed genuine enough though. His contempt for her was obvious, but Morris sensed it went even deeper than Ware displayed. Caused by his great friendship for Hislop? Maybe he was a sort of mentor to Stuart when they were young and felt responsible for him in some way? Something about Ware caused him unease…

Morris met his son in the Doublet at six thirty and they had a couple of pints. It was Kevin's turn to cook so he left early and Morris stayed on a bit to think and chat with the regulars a while. He went outside, lit up a cigarette and phoned Stuart. Hislop was not able to come to the pub as he was heading off to a play in town in half an hour. Morris mentioned his meeting with Ware and asked if there had been any news, or contact with his wife.

'Naw- nothing at all. Anne phoned again, half cut as usual, asking too. She is really worried. I told her you were trying to make some enquiries and was trying to help, but if we could get nowhere, we would get the police officially involved. I did not mention Frazer-is that right?'

'Aye- just leave his name out of it for the moment. I don't want her panicking and phoning the police. Anyway- I'll meet her hopefully tomorrow. I didn't realise you and William were so tight. Pretty forceful bloke in his opinions…'

'Yes, we go way back. He phoned after your visit and mentioned you and him had talked about Liz a lot. He is a good pal. Being a few years older than me he was always trying to give me advice. Sort me out-lead me down the academic path-that sort of thing. Almost like brothers I would say-and still the case.'

"What do you mean, sort you out? He mentioned you had some troubles?'

'Well yes, I did –mostly family stuff. I was heading down the hooligan road. He said he had been there too and nudged me away from trouble. The first time I met him in fact was when I was in a pretty violent fight. He stopped it, took me aside and we talked. By the time I was 16, instead of being in jail, I was starting to stay home and study. Much to my surprise I found I was quite smart- or at least a lot smarter than I thought I was. I was determined to emulate him and get to Glasgow Uni.'

'How did he get on with Liz?" Morris asked, matter of factly. 'By the way, is Ware, or was he, married at all?'

'No, never been. He liked Liz, in fact they generally got on well. But he was always sort of looking at her. Judging her almost- looking for a wrong move- something like that. It was a bit uncomfortable at times- a bit weird. I do sort of feel he wanted to find a flaw, but she was just too nice. I told you that on our last meeting when Liz was there at the Shish Mahal- William was pretty cold- no, very cold- towards Liz. He knew about her affair by then.'

'Did he specifically accuse her, or anything?' Morris said.

'No, not like that. I told him not to mention it- that it was my responsibility. He didn't, but he was sneering at her throughout the meal and dropping innuendos every few minutes. He seemed even angrier with her than I was. I had to tell him to take it easy when we were in the toilets. It was getting embarrassing. Liz looked at me and scowled a couple of times- but never said anything to Willie- she is as bad at me at confronting things. What an awful night.'

'So William never made a move on Liz, or vice versa?' Morris asked cautiously.

'No, no. Nothing like that, 'Stuart said shaking his head. 'He was a confirmed bachelor. We were all just good friends. Willie had a couple of short term girlfriends and the four of us would all go out together, but they never lasted too long. To be honest I think he fancied her…no, that's not the word, I mean sort of respected her might be more apt- but he never made a move. Remember - we are best pals- I don't think he would disrespect me that way. Why? Did he say he did?' Hislop asked and even on the phone Morris could sense Hislop's unease.

'No he didn't. Not at all. Anyway. Best go Stuart. Keep your fingers crossed for a call, or a knock on the door… and enjoy the play.'

'Hello-is that Roy Shorrocks?' Morris enquired down the phone from the lounge in his flat when he got back from the pub.

'Hold on a sec,' came the reply, 'Dad, it's for you,' said a squeaky Essex accented voice.

A few seconds later there was a short, sharp cough. 'Hello, Roy Shorrocks'

'Ah, hello Mr. Shorrocks. My name is Sam Morris and I'm phoning about the Airbnb booking you had in Glasgow three weeks ago in Wilton street. Can you spare a moment?'

'Off great Western Road? Yeah, I remember that one. Nice flat. Is there a problem?' came the reply. 'I paid, through my account I'm sure.'

'Sorry, it has nothing to do with that,' Morris suddenly realised he could not just start talking about Liz disappearing. The guy would think he was a suspect- which he was, but this was not the way to go about it. He needed a bit of diplomacy.

'Eh, it's something a bit personal. I'm not from Airbnb or anything, I just wonder if you could go through the meeting you had with Liz Hislop the host?'

'What are you talking about?' Shorrocks replied, a slightly surprised and questioning tone evident in his reply. 'She let me in – told me how things worked and left. Who are you anyway?'

'Sam Morris. Actually a friend of her husband. I probably should not have put you in the spot but, well, Liz went missing on the same day, or the day after, and I'm just trying to help my pal out before we have to make it official with the police. So if you can tell me anything at all it might help trace her.'

'Oh, I see. Well ok, that's different. Bad. Let me think back. I don't remember too much about it. I'm in Glasgow a lot and go to whichever Airbnb that is free and a good price. I…"

'Sorry to interrupt', Morris said quickly. 'You said you come to Glasgow often? Are you coming again soon? It might be better if we meet. It's a bit awkward on the phone'

'Coming tomorrow, in fact. I guess we could meet up for a while after my interviews. I hope I can help, but doubt it…'

Decent guy, thought Morris. Immediately taking to this Roy Shorrocks.

'How does a couple on me in one of Glasgow's most famous pubs sound?'

Shorrocks laughed. 'Are you a mind reader, or something? That sounds great after a day of travelling and interviews. I've been looking for a good Glasgow pub as well. Do you know any?

'The Doublet is my local and a good place for a chat,' Morris said.

'The Doublet?!" Shorrocks laughed down the phone. 'I know it. Good place. I had a crazy day with some women there a couple of months ago - good at the time but I think best we don't meet there if you don't mind- it could be awkward if she is there.'

Morris laughed too. 'Ok- sure. I understand.' They arranged to meet at the Horseshoe at six on the next evening being in the center and close to Shorrocks' area of business and not too far from the Airbnb he had booked.

'I appreciate this a lot', said Morris after giving Shorrocks directions to the Shoe.

'No worries matey. See you in the pub. Be warned, I'll be very thirsty…'

After his call to Canvey island Morris had phoned Anne Smith and asked to meet. She had wanted to chat about it all down the phone, but Morris thought a face to face meeting would be preferable. Apart from anything else he had not seen her for a few months and thought a night out would do him good and maybe her too. He passed on his condolences about her husband's accident and then asked quickly.

'Tell you what-lets meet in the Chip bar and have a drink and a meal after. Sound good?'

'That sounds great. The Chip -marvelous. It's a great bar.'

There was a pause. 'And how is Linda doing? Anne asked.

'Oh, we split up about a year ago,' replied Morris.

'Oh. I'm sorry to hear that,' she said. Morris considered Anne for a few moments. He had enjoyed her company when they had met before. Blonde, small, busty, vivacious, extremely down to earth and an intelligent girl. But the mention of Linda had also got him thinking about her too. The flashback came again. He arranged to pick Anne up at her place the next evening and head off to the Ubiquitous Chip in Ashton Lane. He got her address in White Street in Partick and put down the phone. A fairly productive day he concluded and therefore he should be Calvinistically rewarded for his efforts with another pint, or two, he smiled to himself. Morris went through to the living room where his son looked up from his computer with a look of anticipation spreading across his face.

'Fancy a quick Jack and coke son before dinner?'

The following evening after a walk in the park with Kevin and his dog, Berny, and an update call to Frazer, Morris showered longer than usual and got his best clothes on. He remembered this was how it used to be with Linda.

'Going on a date, or something?' asked his son when he got back with some messages from Lidl. "Smells like it from the waft of Old Spice after shave,' he laughed and pretended to cough.

'Cheeky bastard. Not really. I'm taking Anne out for dinner and also ask her about Liz- Stuart's wife who seems to have buggered off somewhere. Stuart is worried about her and I'm trying to help a bit. But, yes, I feel like some company. Been a long time since I went out with someone- Linda in fact- way back. That ok?'

'Sure Dad. It will do you good'. Kevin replied, more seriously.

Morris looked at his son with pride as a small smile spread across his face. He was a man now, no doubt about that.

'I should be home by eleven latest,' he said. 'Maybe a quick one in The Doublet if I'm a bit earlier?

His son agreeing, Morris fastened the last bottom of his shirt, draped his jacket over it and headed out to get a passing taxi on the road. He was feeling pretty good. A cab came along soon enough and he took it to White street in Partick to pick up Anne. He had anticipated getting out and ringing the door bell, but just as he pulled up, she left the close and ran to the taxi before he could get out. She wore a knee length dark blue dress, black shoes a warm smile and carried a black handbag. Her blonde hair streamed behind her as she came towards the taxi. She was sixty Morris knew, but could easily be mistaken for fifty. 'How does she manage that?' Morris muttered and laughed to himself. 'You got a smasher there pal', the taxi driver said with a wee laugh and whistle.

He and Anne arrived at the chip and headed to the bar upstairs. He ordered a lager for himself and Anne a large gin and Tonic.

He passed on his condolences about Ian again, but she just said thank you and there was no immediate further discussion about him, which surprised Morris a little. Close up, Anne looked more haggard than she had appeared from a distance, but Morris could see by her feisty manner that she was trying to relax and enjoy the night out. But the mood changed when Liz's name was mentioned. Morris asked if Anne could tell her the full story of their relationship, stating the usual quip that 'the smallest thing might help.'

Anne swirled around her Gin for a second, took a large gulp, stared out the window and commenced.

'Ok, but I'm still pissed off with her, if she is safe and has not called me. Anyway, we met for the first time at a hairdresser. 1985. I was twenty-five- she was only eighteen, we were in chairs next to each other and just started nattering away and got on like a house on fire. You know what's it like-sometimes you just meet someone and after a few minutes realise you are going to get along with them well. Man, or women...we went for a coffee after and then walked around the shops talking away non-stop. From that first day we were friends and met up regularly. I was older then her of course, but she was mature for her age and sort of... thoughtful about things. She asked a lot of questions, I remember.'

'What about?' Morris could not prevent himself saying, even though he had determined to let Anne's recollections flow without interrupting.

'Well, it's a long time ago...' Anne smiled as she remembered and brushed her hair quickly over her ear. 'But you know, the usual concerns at that age. Men, money career, parents mostly - but we had a lot of laughs too -- don't get me wrong. She had a great sense of humour. The innuendos...very clever girl. We were close, but I got the sense a wee bit that she was trying to learn from me. You probably know from Stuart that she had no brothers- just an older sister- but she seemed to have a funny relationship with her. Diana, that's it. She was five years older than Liz. All the guys liked her, Anne used to say when we talked about it. And yes, it did cross my mind that Liz's sister was about the same age as me. I thought a couple of times that

Liz was probing and asking things so that she could relate to her sister in a better way. Maybe? I didn't think too much about it, but it did cross my mind. I think Liz had a strange relationship with her Dad too, but we never went into much detail. Anyway, we met up regularly at the weekend, initially with other girls. You know the usual- drink, dancing, hunting…' She laughed loudly and looked at Morris directly for an instant. 'Soon though we just used to go out together and went to quieter places so we could talk together in peace. We talked for hours. She was troubled and sort of normal at the same time. It's difficult to explain. She could get easily offended…or more like easily hurt I would say. Even by the slightest thing – she would interpret it as a put down. A bit insecure for sure, but such a nice person beneath her troubles. You know don't you that we met Stuart and Ian at the same time?' she laughed again.

Morris did not know, just tilting his head to the side and raising an eyebrow in automatic confirmation that he didn't.

'Well, I suppose that since we were only out socializing together it was not so unusual for both of us to marry the two guys we met,' she laughed.

Morris had already noticed that Anne's drink was finished, as was his and he ordered another two. He realised he was intensely curious about Liz's background for more than professional reasons. He put it down to the Glasgow culture of fascinated curiosity about other people. Anne too, seemed to be more than happy to recall past days and her relationship with her best friend.

'… you know I didn't like Stuart too much at first,' Anne continued. 'He was close to Ian and you could see they were good pals. Funnily enough, Ian was a bit older than Stuart, like me and Liz. But Ian did all the talking and joking. Stuart mostly stayed silent just saying uncontroversial things. Like 'Yes', Anne laughed again and took a large swig of Gin. 'A bit boring for me. I took a shine to Ian straight away. He was flamboyant and vivacious and confident. I liked him – Anne was not so keen saying he was a bit of a smart arse, which he was in a way, true, but he made me laugh.'

'So she preferred Stuart?' Morris asked.

'Oh yes, definitely. I joked that he was a bit boring, but she said she liked his 'quiet, contemplative way.' and that these guys were better in the long run. Proved correct too…if I had only known then…' she cut herself off suddenly and stared out the window. She surprised Morris by reaching over and touching his arm briefly. It sent shock waves through his body. He realised it had been a year since he had last been touched by Linda and she had been the last women to do so. How he missed a gentle physical contact. Anne suddenly stood up.

'What will you have? Something a bit stronger? I'm having another large one.'

He nodded and decided on a Malt. Anne refused Morris's offer to buy the round and when she came back he noticed a slight swaying in her walk. He surmised that she had had a couple of fortifiers before coming out. She sat down and carried on, looking a little morose.

'...you know she still loved him, right?' she continued, before she had even sat down, looking directly at Morris more often now. 'She did, really. But something terrible had gone wrong. It all started suddenly too. One day he was fine, the next, an iron curtain had gone up. She said she felt that Stuart hated her but would not talk about it, although he came close to it a couple of times she mentioned. It really affected her, being so insecure. Liz said she tried everything and thought he had gone of her physically, so started dressing up sexier than normal- that was my suggestion- but apparently it didn't help much- in fact she was starting to think it was making things worse. She was too scared to confront him about the breakdown. Poor Liz. She cried down the phone so many times...and then gone...nothing.'

Morris immediately recalled Stuart telling him about Liz in his bed with another man and that perhaps she was not as devoted to Stuart as Anne was implying. However, he found he could not tell Anne this-at this moment anyway. It certainly sounded that she did not know about it. Instead he generalized.

'Stuart did mention how she was dressing. To be honest, he thought she was having an affair with some guy and also maybe with Airbnb guests…'

Anne put down her drink and stared at Morris, anger quite clear on her face.

'The stupid fucker. She bloody should have after the way he was treating her. But she tried to convince herself it was just a passing phase of his, even though it had lasted weeks. Airbnb guests? Is he fucking mad? Strangers you mean? No way. I knew her-we talked every day, or did until she suddenly stopped. She would have told me I'm a hundred percent. She just would not have done that anyway-full stop.' She stood up and went to the bar without warning and came back with more drinks. Morris looked down. His glass of Malt was nearly full and he was by no means a slow drinker.

'Let's go and eat after this one?' he suggested quickly seeing that Anne was well on the way.

'We can eat anytime.' Anne said immediately and took another large mouthful of gin. It was then that Morris started to think she had a problem. She didn't want a meal at the Chip? He noticed her hand was clutching her glass in a tight grip. No one was getting it from her. He was a bit unsure what to say. There was social drinking to enjoy life and company. And then there was drinking to forget and fuel an addiction.

Booze- a good servant, but a bad master. Morris looked again at her tight red hued skin and the way she held onto her glass. She was firmly in the latter grouping.

'It's a sad story', he ended up saying. 'But, ok. She suddenly left. She didn't contact you? That's what Stuart is really worried about. She had no family- Diana and her folks died years ago-you were her best friend. I'm worried too, to be honest. Doesn't make sense. I think something bad could have happened to her, don't you? Surely if she did leave for another man, she would have left a note, or communicated to Stuart in some way, or you?'

Anne started sobbing and leaned closer to Morris.

'I told you. I'm sure she wouldn't go with, let alone run off with, another man. But, I'm not sure why she left. She would not even call me, her best friend. It hurt me so much. The last time I spoke to her was when Ian died. Liz was the first person I called. It was weird. She hardly said a word, although I sort of felt she wanted to. Something was on her mind for sure. Then after that, silence. No contact with me, Stuart or anyone it seems. At first I tried to justify the lack of calls by saying she just wanted time to herself, but she had nowhere to go that I can think of and surely she would have given me a call. She grabbed his arm again and cried. 'Bastard Stuart, bastard, why did he do that to her. Bastard. Just like Ian did to me too.'

Morris' curiosity got the better of him. All he knew was what Frazer had told him about Anne throwing her husband out after an apparent argument. 'What happened there, with Ian. He started to ignore you- same thing as Stuart do you mean? So you just threw him out?'

'Started to ignore me alright,' she laughed wildly. 'With a bastard man! He was having an affair with another man. Ha, bastards!' Her eyes danced in fury.

'Oh, I didn't know,' said Morris truthfully. 'I'm sorry. Was that quite recent? What happened?'

'I threw him out the same time as the accident. But I had known something was going on for a while- I found a note from his lover. I even followed him and saw him get in a car with the guy. Frank somebody. Ian tried to dismiss the note as a pretend joke and that nothing was going on, but his guilt was a mile wide. Eventually I had enough and asked him to get out the flat. He didn't even argue, just packed up a few things and left. Hours later he was dead…If I hadn't thrown him out he would still be here…'

'What did Liz think about all that?' Morris asked. 'She told Stuart about it you think?'

'No, she didn't tell Stuart or anyone else. She said it was none of her business. She tried to reassure me as I had expected, saying she was sure Ian loved me and it was just a mistake. I think I was sort of hoping Ian would come round and I could sweep it all under the carpet and continue as before. A few days before Ian died we were all out for a meal. Ian was distraught, hardly said a word. Then, three days later, he was dead...'

She stopped suddenly and looked at Morris in the eye and held it. Tears started to well up in her eyes. 'I don't want to eat Sam. Take me home now. Stay with me. Just hold me please...please hold me...'

Morris got home at seven in the morning and got a couple of hours more sleep. He had phoned his son from Anne's place and told him he wouldn't make the Doublet. When Kevin woke at ten, Morris brought him a coffee and received a quizzical look, but no comments. Kevin sat up sipped his coffee and reached for his phone. Morris went up to the shops, bought rolls, square sausages and the National and made a coffee and sat in the lounge on returning- glancing through the paper. He put the newspaper down and decided to have a think. He tried to summarise Liz's disappearance, hoping it would clarify things a bit, at least in his own mind.

'Stuart and Liz in love. She shags another man on their bed. Why? Who? Don't know yet. Stuart's best pal, William? No. Unlikely. Too close to Stuart to betray him. She goes to meet Airbnb guy on the day she is last seen. More shagging-ran off with the guy? No. Shorrocks sounds innocent enough- but we will see what he says when we meet. Liz disappears.

Stuart had gone to Stirling to meet his best pal for a piss up and solace. Stays night – Ware confirms, but not yet police – but don't doubt it. Right. Stuart gets home. No Liz. Gone. No contact since. Anne - her best friend also no contact. Strange, that one. Gone with her lover? Why no communication as such? Could be she wants to make a clean break with everyone, or she is dead? Both possible. No other family - no contact. Parents and sister dead. Stuart a murderer? Don't think so, but Shipman probably seemed a nice, caring, family doctor too… Liz and Stuart both seemed to have some problems when they were young? Yes. Maybe that's why they were happy together? Probably got a lot to do with it. But then why does she start shagging around? Must be a reason, although trying to explain human sexual behaviour was like trying to untie a knot only to see another one form. Maybe Stuart not telling the whole truth and nothing but the truth?' Morris reached over and had a sip of coffee. 'Yes, that could well be the case. Maybe Liz found *him* with another woman? Yes, maybe that could have happened. Or man? This Ian guy was gay it seems. He and Stuart were good pals. Him?' Morris shrugged, but again his instincts tended towards dismissing this possibility. 'Liz may well be dead and Ian too. Coincidence? Probable, but again cannot be dismissed. Ian- Hit and run. Accident? Maybe not- the killer fled the scene so was there something to hide…Anne? No, she had an alibi. His gay lover? That sounded a possibility. He needed to talk with Anne again and see if she had any more information on this Frank guy- that he could pass on to Frazer to check. He let out a long breath of air and shook his head. 'This is a bit of a bastard to figure out at the moment,' he thought, then stood up determinedly. 'You'll get there though, you'll get there…'

After dozing off again for a couple of hours in the afternoon, Morris met Roy Shorrocks in the Horse Shoe Bar as arranged, recognizing him from his Airbnb profile photo. Shorrocks had a cheerful, glass half full look on his face. It matched the impression of him gauged from their telephone call. He was of medium height, had a large beer belly and wore glasses on his bald head.

'Roy Shorrocks? he asked, so confident he was already presenting his hand to shake.

Shorrocks turned towards him and laughed. 'Correct. Is an English man so obvious?'

Morris laughed back as they shock hands, got a couple of pints in and sat down.

'I don't know if there is much I can tell you' Shorrocks immediately said. 'I was thinking about that trip on the drive up, but not much to say, I'm afraid.'

'Sure, no problem,' Morris reassured. 'If you can just tell us about your meeting and any impressions you had of Liz the host, that would be great. I'm just following up on things. She is still missing by the way.'

'That's awful,' said Shorrocks, with genuine concern as it seemed to Morris, who again was impressed with the guy.

'Well. I set off early, got here about half two, three, I think it was…first time at that Airbnb. I found Wilton street easy enough though, took my bag from the car and she was waiting outside the flat. The door was opened – smelt good and looked like she had been cleaning it. We shook hands and she took me in. Looked around. Nice place. She explained how everything worked, contact numbers for problems and such like and that was about it…all normal enough. An attractive lady for sure.'

'Ok. Thanks,' Morris said. 'That was probably the very day she left her husband, so as a friend I'm trying to help him. No one has seen her since you met- that's why I needed to talk with you.'

'I was the last person to see her as far as you know then? Shorrocks asked. 'Right. I hope she is ok. She seemed a nice lady. And in case you are wondering- I left the flat straight after and was doing interviews all day and the next up until just before nine at night both nights. I can verify it all if you want, so no need to have the police arrest me,' he laughed, somewhat nervously.

Morris nodded. 'I know it sounds daft, but what were your impressions of her? Did she look ok, act ok?

I'm just trying to figure her state of mind, since she buggered off that same day, or the next. You think for a minute or two-I'm going for a piss…'

On returning Shorrocks sipped his pint and continued.

'Thinking again about it. As I say she was very nice. Polite and friendly. But after she went into her bag to give me the keys she did look slightly distracted and jittery. Worried even. Hard to put my finger on it. I'm not sure, but she seemed to read something in her bag- two of her fingers were holding what looked like a bit of paper, but I couldn't see clearly. She did look like she had received a shock. After that she didn't overly rush me, but at the same time I felt she did not want to hang around too long. She looked flustered.

'That could be important, yes' said Morris already thinking of the possibilities. 'Was she in a rush to get somewhere, meet someone?' he pondered and wondering what she had noticed and read in her bag that had seemed to change her demeanor so quickly.

'So you just stayed the two nights and left? 'he asked.

'Correct. Did my interviews and was back in Canvey by ten pm two days after getting here. It's a long drive. I'm divorced, just me and my daughter, so I try and get back down as quick as I can. Can't fly though- I have a phobia about heights. Anyway, when

I left I just put the key through the letter box as she instructed.'

'So I take it you are heading back tomorrow? Fancy a wee pub tour and a curry after?' Morris suggested.

'I do indeed Sir. Will we have one more here though? Some bar...magic. I'll remember this one.'

When Morris got home that night, slightly pissed, he poured himself a small malt and went into the sitting room and sat down feeling maudling. He kept the room dark and fixed his gaze out the window as he thought, He let his mind drift as it wanted, refusing to interrupt it as it contemplated the complicated and often toxic nature of human's relationships with each other 'Human nature, human instinct, human betrayal, jealousy, lust, revenge, bitterness, spite. We have it all in spades...It's funny how we always judge others behaviour to a much higher moral standard than we do our own,' He thought of a few examples in his own life. 'Could be the hub of it all...we think others should act how we think we *should* behave.' He remembered watching true crime documentaries and being astounded at the reasons people killed each other, especially the planned murders where people walked around calmly for months as they plotted to kill another human- and very often a human they knew- or had even loved before. 'Jesus,' he uttered quietly, 'what a frightening species we are.' He downed his drink. Through the window and over the other side of the Kelvin river, only one light was one in the otherwise darkened tenements. He felt a melancholy connection with it. He stared for a minute wondering how the people in that wee room were getting on. What was their untold stories? Through the viewed window he saw a shadow move briefly across the dim light. He wondered what the owner was thinking of at that moment and realised with a shudder how little humans really knew of someone else's thoughts as we all acted out the pretense of human interaction on a daily basis. He stood up slowly, turned from the window and headed for his room looking forward to the forgetfulness of sleep.

Morris woke the next morning his mind still full of the conundrums he had been contemplating before bed. Realising that alas, he had still yet to figure out the world, he headed to the kitchen to make a coffee. Peering through the kitchen window he saw it was a decent day, with a pale blue sky and judging by the bending of the tree leaves, a light wind. 'That's four days in the last month,' he thought, concluding only half in jest that no further proof for Global Warming was needed. He had a sudden image of a climate conference, the solemn scientist speaking at the lectern. 'In Glasgow, in June and July this year, there were four days when the temperature was over thirty-two degrees and the sun was out for more than two hours a day.' (The attendees gasp)' Ladies and gentleman - I rest my case.' Morris grinned to himself on leaving the kitchen and poked his head into Kevin's room, but he was sound asleep. He would give him an hour. His thoughts drifted yet again to Linda. On the spur of the moment and surprising himself he reached for the phone and dialed her number in Lochinver. He had not spoken to her in a year- since the fall out. Maybe it was just the mood he was in that morning, or subconscious conclusions from the previous night's musings, but he decided his jealousy and his reaction to what happened between them had been excessive and rather pathetic, if truth be told. He took a deep breath and waited for her to pick up…hoping to get rid of that wall in his mind. He waited, but there was no answer. Disappointed, but glad he had had the balls to at least try to contact her, he ended the call. 'Soon', he muttered, with some determination, 'soon…'

CHAPTER 4

Stuart Hislop had gone for an early morning walk in Kelvingrove park, taking advantage of the clement weather. Back in the flat, he changed into his slippers and put the kettle on. The phone went. He was a bit surprised, it being 7:25am.

'Hello…hello. Who's speaking…its Quita Warner here…'

Hislop remembered the name, but took a second to place it.

'Quita? Liz's friend?' He was aware of the rush of blood and his heart rate increasing.

'Yes, yes. Is that you Stuart? Is she in? I know it's a bit early, but thought I'd try.'

Hislop was caught off guard. 'What to say?' But he felt a desperate need to know what Quita had to say.

'I'm afraid she is not here. In fact, she left unexpectedly a couple of weeks ago,' he said.

'Left? A holiday, or something you mean? Warner asked.

'No, left for good it seems. She has not phoned. Nothing. She hasn't been in contact with you has she?' he replied.

'Well, it's strange. I got a call from her last night about midnight. She just said my name and mumbled something and then the line went dead. I'm sure it was her. Thing is she sounded scared the way she said my name. Maybe I'm being paranoid, but she sounded frightened about something.'

Hislop's head was spinning.

'Listen, listen' he realised he was nearly shouting. 'You are sure it was her? Please, its important.'

'Ok, ok, take it easy' Quita replied. 'I'm sure it was her and I'm sure she is ok. Just a bit worried, thought it best to call. To be honest, I think she was drunk as well.'

"You don't understand. Sorry, sorry. She disappeared. Went to see an Airbnb guest and then gone. She is missing, the police know, I have a friend looking for her. Its serious, so any news…'

'Wow. I see. Ok. Missing officially. Bloody hell. What happened?' Warner asked anxiously.

Hislop tried to compose himself and gave her a summary of the last time he had seen Liz.

'You said she went to see an Airbnb guest and that was the last you saw her. When was this exactly?' Warner asked when Hislop had finished.

'Two and a bit weeks ago. June 16th. Why do you need to know? Does it help?'

'Could do. Because I saw her around then. We met…'

Hislop interrupted. 'You saw her?'

'Yes, hold on, I'll check. Yes, here it is on phone calls. She phoned on the 16th- ah the same day- and we met in the afternoon.'

'Thank God, thank God,' Hislop spluttered.

'Why is that so important?' Quita asked.

'Well it shows she was ok, for a start. We all thought something happened to her. She has had no further communication with anyone as far as we know till the call to you. So she is alive. I thought…ok. But she sounds distressed you say? Look, if she calls again, tell her we are worried sick. Anything she wants I will do to help. Anything. Whatever is the problem, we can fix it. Hey, you have the number she phoned you on? '

'Yes, of course, but its dead every time I try to call. That's why I phoned your number.' Warner called over the numbers after Hislop had got a pen and paper.

'Look Quita- thanks for the call, but I need you to meet someone- a friend of mine. Sam Morris. He is helping me find her. Can you meet today if he can make it? '

'Well ok, of course, no problem if it helps'. She gave her number. 'Any time is ok and sorry for what has happened. I'm sure she is ok Stuart. Don't worry.'

'That's great, thanks so much Quita. Just thinking. You said you met her. Where was that?'

'Costas coffee shop near Queen street station. We only talked for a wee while. She had a rucksack and said she had to go away. She asked me if would do one thing for her and when I said yes, she just smiled weakly and said that if I ever met you again just to tell you that she loved you. Didn't know what the hell she was talking about…She looked distracted and in a bit of a state. Definitely worried about something.'

Immediately after finishing the call Hislop paced around the lounge for a few minutes, thinking frantically and then phoned Morris. He listened intently as Hislop explained all the details, noted down Quita Warner's contact and the number of the phone Liz had used, had a wash, phoned Quita and agreed to meet at Queen street station at 1pm. He tried Liz's number several times with no success. After a morning walk and some shopping he called Frazer at noon and updated him.

'Well, it seems Liz is probably ok, maybe a bit distressed and lonely – reaching out to a friend, before having second thoughts – but alive still probably, so sounds excellent news.' Frazer summed up.

'Aye. I'm meeting this Quita in an hour at Queens street station. I'm guessing she took a train somewhere. I'll keep you informed, of course.'

'Please do. Try and get her to recall the time of their meeting. We will get a timetable and check departing trains around that time. Might help. I agree that we can reasonably presume she was about to take a train.'

'Good thinking. Yes, that could help a bit. The excitement is coming back. We are on the trail. I'm going to find her. She is alive. Great – and clears Stuart from suspicion. He is worried, but obviosuly relieved as well.'

'Have you tried the number Liz phoned from yet?' Frazer asked.

'Five or six times already. Blank.'

'Ok, give me it though. Technical guys might be able to help' Frazer said.

Morris did so, then told Frazer about Anne telling him that Ian had been having an affair with someone called Frank when she asked him to leave and that he would see if Anne could supply a full name, or any other clue to his identity.'

'Ah, that's interesting. She just mentioned she had asked him to leave- didn't mention anyone else being involved. Could be something right enough- please chase it up Sam if you can.'

Morris ended the call and went for a quick shower. He felt the excitement of his Casino investigation days. An old feeling which he missed. He felt mentally fit, his mind racing in fifth gear. 'Alive!', he concluded- planning possible scenarios in his head as he wet and rubbed his hair vigorously in the shower. Morris send a text when he got to Queen street. The station, recently refurbished looked smart and clean.

Quita Warner had seen his text and looked around waving her hand. Their eyes met and he joined her and they went to a coffee stand. 'I'm sorry,' he started. 'Did we ever meet? I don't recall.,'

'Don't think so,' she replied, smiling. 'Nice to meet the famous casino detective at last.' They both laughed, he shaking his head in embarrassment. Quita had an engaging smile, short auburn hair and light green, darting eyes.

'Ok' Morris said. 'Let's go over this. Liz phoned you late last night. Sounded drunk and worried. That was it…?'

'Yes. I'm afraid that was about all that happened. Probably not much help…I'm sorry.'

'Not at all,' Morris said reassuringly. 'It's just great to know she is alive at least. Stuart was going crazy with worry. He is so relieved to hear the news. But, as you said, she sounds like she is in some sort of trouble. I'm going to try and find her, just in case it is serious. After that, if she decides that she wants no more contact with anyone, I guess that is up to her. Can't figure what the hell has happened to her though. She just ups and leaves. No note, no call – even to her best friend, Anne. Do you know her by the way?'

'Anne? Yes, a bit. Met her a couple of times when I was with Liz. Married to Ian. Lovely man. We used to…'

Morris cut her off.

'Oh, you didn't know? I'm afraid Ian died recently in a car accident. I'm sorry.'

Quita clasped her hands against her cheeks and let out a gasp.

'Oh no, I didn't know. That's terrible. Anne must be distraught…'

'Well yes, of course, but he had left her – she is a bit bitter, but yes, upset too. She is in a bit of a mess. I saw her two days ago...'

'They split up? I spoke to her about a month ago and she never mentioned it? Are you sure?'

'Yes, sure. He left after that – or rather she threw him out, about three weeks ago. He was having an affair.'

'He met another women. Bloody hell. Shows what I know - thought they were still in love. I'm shocked.'

'It wasn't another women…'

Quita looked confused for a moment and then raised her eyebrows. Her mouth opened slightly.

Quita looked confused for a second. 'Oh my Lord. Another man? Anne…'

'Yes, she is a bit bitter to say the least. He was actually killed in a hit and run up at the University hours later after she had thrown him out. Still no one arrested for it.'

'What? You think it was her?!' Quita said in disbelief. 'She has got a temper and is a bit principled, but...'

'No, no, no. The police talked to her and her whereabouts was verified,' Morris replied.

'Poor Anne. Send my love when you see her again- that's awful.'

'Will do,' Morris nodded. 'Now all this was the same time that Liz left, so I don't know what is going on. There seems to be no connection apart from the fact that Liz and Stuart were close friends with Anne and Ian. We will see...Anyway, you met Liz. Remember the time exactly?'

'She phoned me around four in the afternoon and asked me to meet her at Costas in George square at five,' Quita replied concentrating. 'She said she wanted to tell me something. But when we met, she was obviously flustered and didn't tell me anything -just what I told Stuart - to tell him Liz loved him if I saw him. We sat in a corner far away from the door, but she kept looking to see if anyone was coming in. Nervous as hell. She grabbed my hand a couple of times and squeezed it hard. I felt she wanted to tell me something, but couldn't bring herself to say it. I had never seen her in such a state.'

'Ok. You met at five and talked for how long? Then she went straight to the station.'

'Yes. We talked just for maybe ten minutes only. She picked up her rucksack, got up quickly apologised and said she was sorry – maybe she would call later and explain some things. I remember thinking how strange that she had asked to meet as if it was something important and then had not told me anything. I was a bit disappointed and worried as well by her nervousness. I watched her when she left. She went straight to the station.'

'Looks more than likely she caught a train somewhere. I can probably find out the destination since we have the date and time. Good.'

'You don't need to. I was worried enough about her behavior to follow her over a few minutes after she had left. I was going to insist that she told me what the matter was.'

'Ah- did you see which train she got on?' Morris asked.

'Not quite sure, I was less than five minutes behind her –I think I saw her get on a train, but it was far up the platform, not sure. The Inverness train. Five twenty-three. I checked. The previous train was to Dundee at five eighteen. I would say Inverness pretty confidently.' Quita nodded.

'Ok, great. Saves me a bit of work. Thanks. Inverness. Pretty far away as far as Scotland goes.

Figures maybe though, if she was trying to escape from something. Ah, I think she and Stuart used to go up to the Highlands quite often. Think it was the west coast though, not Inverness…'

'She might just have been taking the train to Inverness and going on somewhere from there?' Quita suggested.

'True,' Morris nodded, draining his coffee and starting to stand up. 'The Investigation continues! I'll do my best to track her down and check she is alright at least.' He smiled warmly at Quita, reassuring her that he would update her with anything he found out and thanking her for the meeting and the information she had passed on.

'Thank you. When you find her tell her I'm waiting and I love her.' She said and gathered her things as she stood up to leave,

Morris paid the bill at the counter and walked to the adjoining Buchanan street Underground. As he moved down the escalator he thought of Liz Hislop huddled away up north somewhere, frightened and lonely. His determination to find her increased.

CHAPTER 5

Liz Hislop got out of bed and looked out of the caravan window. Enard Bay was flat with a blue/grey hue and a spear of reflected light split across its horizon. She made a coffee, staring into the grey mug as she poured in the water. 'Another day in paradise,' she smiled sarcastically. 'How long had it been now since I left? She counted. Three weeks ago exactly. Out and no contact, Ian had said. She had come to the most remote spot that she had thought of. She reached for her phone and read his message yet again…

'Liz. I am deadly serious. I'm walking. No time for more. Just left Willie. Lost it. You are in danger. Leave your place. NOW! Serious. DO NOT TELL ANYONE WHERE YOU GO. I'll contact later and explain all.'

Liz remembered exactly when she saw the message. It was a day she would never forget. She was on her way to the shops not long before three in the afternoon, after having given the keys to her Airbnb guest, and had opened her phone and saw the message from the early morning at 05:20. She had been asleep when it was sent. She had stared at the message in disbelief. It did not say exactly, but the implication was that Willie- must be William Ware she figured- had wanted to harm her. What for? He had been nasty to her recently- but to actually harm her? And that message had come on top of the note she had found in her bag when she was talking to the Airbnb guest at Wilton st.

'I know and you know you are a Hoare and one day very soon you will pay. How could you you fucking bitch?'

It was a drunken scrawl and she had no idea how it had got in her bag or how long it had been there, but it had scared the hell out of her.

And then just half an hour later she had opened Ian's message. Ian would not say such things lightly. The final nail arrived thirty minutes after getting home when Anne had phoned with the news of Ian being killed in a car accident. She couldn't believe what was happening. It had felt like she was being hit with hammer blows from all sides. She had not told Anne about the note or phone message, or that Ian had been at Wares house earlier, - it would have seemed selfish to be talking about that her while her best friend had just lost her husband in a car accident. After the call, she had sat for a moment thinking of the note, Ian's message and his death, Stuarts recent treatment of her and Ware's sneering looks and comments to her at the dinner at the Shish. At that moment she had decided to leave and immediately without word and before Stuart got back from Stirling. She needed to get away from everyone- now. She decided to tell Anne at a later date, if and when Liz had figured out what the hell was going on. She had packed some things into a rucksack and left. She had walked through Kelvingrove park thinking where to go. Somewhere remote she had concluded. As Liz now remembered that day she shivered and held her warm coffee close. Outside the grey clouds rolled rapidly across the sky threatening rain. Ian had been killed by a Hit and Run Anne had said. She had seen references to it in the papers after. The driver had still not been found. Liz sat upright, going through it all yet again. Maybe Ian had been killed deliberately since the driver had not stopped? Ian warned her and next minute he is dead? Ian had said he had left Willie- maybe Willie had followed him and run him down. Why though? She wanted to get out of the caravan and just walk and think. Find a solution, but she could not figure out what to do. She thought yet again of going to the police, but what could they do? She had been warned - but hard to explain to the police why someone would want to kill her, when she had no idea herself. The police would give her short thrift, she was sure. She was worried about Willie, but would have to prove to the police why this highly respected Professor would want to harm her- and she didn't have a bloody clue. She was scared as she was when young and could not turn to anyone. Back then, she had met Anne who understood everything. How she longed to phone her. She shook her head, dismissing the idea. It was her husband who had warned her and he had said contact no one. She had resisted that suggestion until late last night after too much to drink. She had found a half bottle of Gin and an old phone in the cupboard and charged it up. Drunk and melancholy she had phoned Quita, but had instantly regretted it and ended the call. No way Quita could be part of a plot to harm her, but it was not right to involve her. Meeting her at Costas before she left had been a mistake, borne out of desperation to try and communicate her problems to someone who could not be involved. As if somehow Quita could have provided all the answers. Daft idea. Liz determined not to phone anyone again, but she couldn't just wait here forever. She knew she had to sort it out herself. 'who would want to harm her and why?' she thought for the umpteenth time. 'Stuart?' Why had he been so nasty lately? His sudden and strange, cold behaviour. His sarcastic comments and the loathing look she could see behind them. 'But why, why, why…?' She stared out the caravan window again. The sea was calm and the wind light through the darkening skies. She determined to go out, at least for a while, before the rain came. Quickly she grabbed her coat and left the caravan. She would walk to the River Inver and back maybe finding answers along the way. She had never felt so alone in her life.

Julia Sinclair also had anxious thoughts that day. From her flat near Charing Cross she looked out the window yet again, fearing a visit from the police. She had wanted to tell them what had happened, but Colin, her lover, had insisted that she could not and that it would all pass without further issues if she just waited a while. 'Trust me,' she remembered him saying over the phone. Mr Colin Worth-big shot-with his OBE-and airs and graces. They had not dared meet since, until he had sorted it all out. He said he knew exactly what to do, which was basically nothing. She had argued that it was an accident. Now, she remembered it all yet again. ... The man she had run over was being chased by someone and had just run out onto the street next to the University and she hadn't had a chance to avoid him. He had been looking over his shoulder and not seen Julia coming. It had been horrible. He had flipped right over and landed on his head. She knew he was dead. She had stopped for a second and started to get out the car. She remembered hearing a dog parking somewhere, intruding on the deathly silence. The other guy had looked at the dead body lying in the road, hesitated, turned and ran. He was very tall and had brown trousers on, that's all she could remember. Sinclair had felt panic sweep through her, got back in the car and drove off. After, she had felt terrible and guilty-compounded by not reporting it to the police. But Colin had said because she had not stopped the police would want to dig further, to see if she had been drinking for example and would want to know exactly where she had been. That was trouble for him, his reputation and his business. He had very strongly insisted she keep quite. When he had asked if anyone had seen her after the accident she had instinctively said no. Something inside had told her best to keep that one quiet. So she had had not told him about the man with the brown trousers, or the old man who had seen her briefly as she sped past Park Road and who she figured might have heard the accident, or figured it out from the news reports. It had been three weeks but the police had not traced her. Both witnesses had not come forward it seemed, or rather she hoped. The old man had looked at her in such a strange way though. Two days after the accident she had sold the blue Mercedes. Colin had given it to her as a present and told her to get rid of it. She kept the cash and he was yet to ask for it back. Since the accident, she had had not been near Kelvinbridge area or met up with Colin. He seemed quite happy with that arrangement. She was sure he wanted their relationship to end. The bastard- just when she needed him the most. She cursed herself again for falling for a married man. Now she felt trapped, anxious and guilty. She thought again of trying to convince Colin that it was better to go to the police. It was the right thing to do, even if he was determined that she shouldn't. A thought suddenly came to her. Well, if he wanted her silence- he was a wealthy man and….

William Ware was pacing around the lounge in his house thinking frantically. At first the death of Ian had seemed the answer to all his wishes. The hit and run had been a lucky break. He was out the way and thank God for that. He had read the papers avidly. The old women whose car Ian had run into had shot off - the police had not found her and he certainly was not going to volunteer any information. He didn't think the driver had noticed him too much, but was still worried. Being six foot seven, with shoulder length hair and his corduroy trousers and his Glasgow flat just up the road they would soon trace him. Sleeping with Ian had been the worst mistake of his life. Some urge had got a hold of him… he couldn't explain. He shook his head and drew on his cigarette. When Ian had left his flat Ware had followed him intending to plead with him, or threaten him if necessary, not to tell anyone about what had happened. Ware had seen Ian texting and was worried that maybe it was about what had just happened. It probably wasn't Anne he was messaging since he had just been thrown out so it was probably Liz since Ware had been ranting about what he was going to do to her. What did he message? Maybe nothing, maybe everything. Then would she have told Stuart? Hopefully nothing as they were barely talking to each other, but on the other hand after his performance at the dinner at the Shish that night…? Maybe she had figured out too that the note he slipped into her bag had been written by him. Liz then might have relished the prospect of telling Stuart. It would break Ware's heart if Stuart knew about him and Ian. But she had left just a few hours later after the accident. Off with her lover maybe, the slut, but had she told Stuart anything before she left? It seemed not. Stuart had not mentioned or hinted anything about Ware sleeping with Ian. So that was a break. But she would be bound to tell him when she came back, or contacted Stuart again. Maybe there was still a chance if he could just get to the bitch and shut her up. Stuart had called and told him that Liz was alive and had headed up to Inverness, but had still to make contact, Quita Warner being the only one so far as far as Stuart knew. She was still alive then, but not communicating. Perfect for the moment. Up in the Highlands somewhere. He had to find her, find out who and what she had told anyone and then shut her up for good. He nodded to himself firmly. He would kill for Stuart; he knew he could do it. He decided to call Quita Warner, the friend Stuart had told him Liz had met and spoke to. He did not know her, but managed to get her number after an on line search helped by her name being quite distinctive. After some pleasantries where he explained he was a good friend of Stuart, he asked her about Liz.

'…yes, I was talking to Stuart. He is still really worried despite you telling him that Liz was ok, although he is upset about Liz sounding desperate about something. It's really strange the whole thing. She didn't tell you anything in that call why she disappeared up north?'

'No.' Warner said 'She called me, I met her expecting her to tell me something, but she didn't mention anything important really. She was worried about something though, that's for sure. - just didn't specify.'

Ware smiled to himself. 'It's just that Stuart is my pal, so I would like to help him find her. What can we do, do you think?'

'You know Sam Morris?' Katie said and without waiting for a reply: 'He has been helping Stuart quite a lot. I actually met him at Queen street station. It's nice he is so concerned. I told him that it was pretty certain that Liz had taken the Inverness train. I'm ninety per cent sure I saw her get on it.'

'Hey that's great,' But his mind was aghast. Morris – the nosy bastard he had met in the University coffee shop. He was a sharp cookie. Damn. Damn. Shite. He was still poking his nose around. 'I see -he will probably be looking for her. That's fine then. Ok, so all in good hands. Great. If you hear anything though Quita, please give us a call. I'll only be able to sleep peacefully when I know she is back home safely with Stuart. Thanks love.'

He ended the call. He was worried that he had not sounded too convincing at the end. 'Aye, I'll only be able to sleep peacefully when I find her and shut her up for good,' he had really thought, deciding there and then that it was time to take a trip up to the Highlands and remembering Stuart and Liz normally headed to the west coast after Inverness.

CHAPTER 6

'You went up to the Highlands quite a lot I remember?' Morris asked on the phone to Hislop. He had told him about the probable Inverness destination from Queen street. 'And from there over to the West coast often? Anywhere special?'

'Once or twice a year we went up. Train to Inverness to enjoy the scenery and then hired a car just outside the station. Drove over to the west coast, but went all around I'm afraid. Nowhere special, although we did stay at your neck of the woods, Lochinver, a few times. I guess if she was hiding she would go somewhere else though. I don't know…Listen Sam. Maybe we should just leave her alone. I don't want to waste your time and she is alive at least. Maybe she just doesn't want to see me again and I have to accept that…Maybe she is with a guy after all.'

'Doubt it, but I understand and I'll leave it if you want, but it does seem that she is scared and troubled about something. Personally, I would think it best to at least find her, see what the problem is and if all ok and, if she wants us to, leave her alone. If not, try and help her. What do you think?'

'I know, I know. But I can't think what the trouble might be, so keep telling myself there is nothing too serious to worry about. She just doesn't want to see me again. But you are right, there must be something. Ok. Let's try and find her at least. If you go up north can I come too? Might be able to help…'

'Aye, sure. Would be glad to have company. Haven't been up there for a while. We can all do with a wee break, I'm sure. I'll try and meet Linda one night though by myself while we are around Lochinver. I have been a coward with her Stuart. Pathetic. That's if she will even see me…'

'Yeah, I know about regrets for sure. I never really knew why you broke up. Hope it can be mended if that's what you want?'

'Damn thing is - I don't know if it is. Usual women confusion, but I do think of her all the time- like you do with Liz, no doubt. Ok. I suggest we go as soon as possible and follow the route you took the last time you were up. Who knows- we might get lucky. Alisdair Frazer might give us some location on the phone she used too, which would help. Head off day after tomorrow? Actually I'll see if Kevin can get a few days off work too. Would be good for him to get up there again and he got on with Linda well…Just a thought…Is Anne still in contact with you?'

'Yes, still phoning regularly. She was really happy to find out Liz is ok, but a bit peeved that she had not contacted her after I told her that Liz had called Quita…Anne asked about three times where Liz was, even though I said I didn't know.'

Morris thought for a moment his mind throwing possibilities around.

'Listen Stuart, sounds a bit weird, but maybe not tell everyone about what's happening. Something might be up, we don't know what and we don't know who is involved. Let's keep the information between ourselves. At least until we find out a bit more. Ok?'

'Trust no one you mean?' 'Spoken like a real Surveillance man. Everyone is guilty until proven innocent… But I get your point. Anyway, only her and Willie have called recently.'

'Ware, your pal from Stirling Uni?'

'Yes, the guy you met. He has been a big support these last few weeks. Especially when I was really down.'

'Well ok, but let's keep the information going out to the minimum. Did you tell him Liz has been found to be at least safe for the moment? He knows about the meeting with Quita.'

'Can't remember exactly what I said, but I think I did tell him that Quita had phoned and it looked like she had gone up to Inverness. I'll say nothing in the future if you think it's best. If he phones I'll just say I'm going for a break by myself- down to London or something. Ok?'

'Aye, good idea. Ok pal. I'll phone tomorrow and book the tickets for Thursday morning. Looking forward to it actually.'

Morris, Kevin and Hislop departed Queen street early Thursday morning. It was a fine day and the trip passed pleasantly. Kevin mostly looked out the window while Morris and Hislop were in good cheer, with the sense of adventure and a common purpose adding to their camaraderie. They arrived in Inverness at lunchtime and hired a car from Hislop's usual rental and headed off towards the west coast. They stopped in Beauly for fish and chips and then drove straight to Ullapool to the Royal Hotel Morris had pre- booked. The same hotel as Stuart and Liz had stayed in on their last trip, six months before and indeed, on several other occasions. The staff recognized Stuart and one or two asked where Liz was and confirming, when asked, that they had not seen her at all since she was last there with him.

Friday morning Morris and Hislop woke early and went down for breakfast- Kevin joining them half way through it. Morris glanced at his weary looking son and recalled his own youth when he would feel sluggish all day until the night closed in and he was transformed into an energetic, social and lustful predator. He had a wee laugh to himself. He felt a little of that hunting instinct now. There was someone to track down- something to solve and accomplish. It was a good feeling and a change from the monotony of Ground Hog day retirement. He pushed his chair back making an irritating screeching noise. Kevin looked like he had been tazered and grimaced.

'Right. Let's get going,' Morris said. 'We will follow your usual path Stuart. Up towards Lochinver and we will ask around there. Stay a night or two. Kev, remember Lochinver? Been a while…' Kevin nodded and smiled.

'You will see Linda maybe, or I can?' he asked, perking up a bit.

'Sure. I was planning on that if she is ok with it. I'm sure she would love to see you at any rate.'

The three of them went upstairs, packed and checked out and headed up north.

In the early morning in her caravan asleep, sounds from outside the caravan started to wonder into Liz's dreams. There was a strong wind pushing in from the Minch which rattled the loose door of the caravan on occasion, but there was something else – a quiet movement somewhere outside. Liz awoke in a fright. She sat up and listened intently, not moving. She heard it again. Someone was moving around the caravan. She had a rush of panic, got quickly out of bed and checked the door was locked. There was a moment of silence and then she heard the movement again. It was just outside the door. Then a bump on the side of the caravan and another. Someone was trying to find a way in. Liz looked round in desperation. Not knowing what else to do she grabbed a small knife from the kitchen area and stood by the door waiting. She could feel a thin film of sweat on her brow despite the cold. She now heard more movement. It sounded like there were two persons outside. She moved slowly to the curtains and drew them slightly aside. At first she saw nothing, although she could still hear movement. She thought of Stuart and longed for him. Then from the corner of the window two sheep came into view. Liz breathed out and almost laughed in relief. She sat down and shook her head. But there was another nagging feeling stuck in her thoughts and now coming to the fore. She could tell she had been dreaming of it all night. The call to Quita –that was it. First she had met her in strange circumstances in the coffee shop and she had seen Quita just as she was getting on the train to Inverness standing looking for her. She had more than likely seen Liz too. Then she had called her and cut off the call after a few seconds the other night. So, probably Quita would have phoned Stuart and told him about the strange call from her and he would have told her she was missing. She would have said she had seen her leaving to Inverness- just as she and Stuart had done numerous times in the past. So- for God's sake- he would have a rough idea of where she was. And she was staying in Lochinver. And the phone-bugger. Maybe she gave Stuart the number and he went to the police and maybe they could trace it to a location, even though it was not her phone?

'Idiot.' she chastised herself. If instead of sheep it had been someone intend on harming her there would have been no escape. She decided immediately that she had to move on. She almost cried in desperation. 'Where can I go?' As she packed she considered destinations, thinking that a remote hide out might not be the best place to be when someone is looking to find and harm you. Somewhere public then...? There was still no one she could trust. She finished packing her rucksack and went quickly out to the car parked behind the caravan and out of sight of the one-way track road passing by. It was a clear, silent morning. The sea was calm and she tried to quieten her frantic nerves in tune. She sat for a few minutes more, trying to figure where to go. She turned on the engine, went into reverse gear and the car inched out from behind the caravan. She had decided to go to the last place anyone would think of if they knew she was in the Highlands. Back to Glasgow, but in a safe, public place- a hotel. She checked the time. 09:05. She had paid for the caravan up until Monday, but decided not to ask for a refund. She had enough problems…

It can be called fate, or coincidence, or bad luck, and all three could apply to the circumstance that caused Morris, Hislop and Kevin all to miss Liz as they passed each other on the road to and from Ullapool. Morris, drifting back to his younger days, had recalled the approaching first glimpse of the magnificent mountain Suilven as they headed north. When he was a wee boy his father had promised six pence to either Morris or his sister to whoever first spotted the mountain appearing. Recounting the story while driving, Morris had laughed to his passengers.

'Ten quid to the first to see Suilven', he announced. Hislop had laughed too as he said. 'Daft bugger. Ok, you are on. Hey Kevin, what's that on your foot? Looks like seagull shite-better wipe it off now…'

'Nice try Stuart,' Kevin laughed too as he continued to emerge from his morning slumbers, but already looking keenly out of the window. Ten quid was ten quid. There were few cars on the road at that time. Had Morris not recalled his father's game with his children, or decided not to talk about it, one of them would surely have seen the car driven by Liz pass by. As it was Morris had slowed down and along with the other two had his eyes firmly fixed to the left awaiting that first glimpse of Suilven. Liz on the other hand, afforded a quick look at the almost stationary car, but, preoccupied with her plans, did not recognise the three passengers whose faces were turned away from her in a hired car. She carried on, not cognisant of who she had just passed. Liz reached Ullapool and decided to stop at a coffee shop or restuarant and plan her next moves with a little more precision. After this she decided she would drive straight to Inverness and hand in the car. The train to Glasgow was around six pm. She entered The Frigate on Shore street and ordered a mug of tea. She gazed out the window, her sight fixed on one of the trawlers moored to the dock as she thought. Several tourists and locals passed through her view. It started to rain slightly, just a light drizzle, though the darkening clouds suggested there was more to come. She did a slight double take and stood up pushing her chair back with a screeching grate that drew her a withering look from an old couple in the corner. She moved quickly to the window and searched to the left and gasped. There striding purposively along the front and away from her was William Ware. Wearing brown corduroys as always, his long hair flowing backwards in the wind. And a helmet in his hand. Yes, it was him. For sure. She remembered the text and the written note. Her mind raced with possibilities, as her heart pounded. 'Why was William Ware, lecturer at Stirling University and Stuarts best friend here of all places? He had never mentioned coming to the Highlands before despite Stuart and Liz's several recommendations. He was by himself too. Something about the way he looked as he disappeared from view unsettled Liz. It was akin to quiet determination as he strode purposively along rather than a relaxing amble along the sea front she surmised. She shivered. She remembered again how Ware had treated her at the Shish meal a few days before she had left. Why had Ian just not told her exactly what the danger was, she cursed for the hundredth time. Ian. Dead man. His warning had been hugely reinforced by his demise. Liz paid her bill and waited at the doorway for a few minutes. She was thankful that she had brought the umbrella from the car after deciding rain had been likely. Her car was parked in the direction that Ware had been walking towards, so she left the café, the umbrella covering her from the shoulders upwards and turned sharply to the left away from where she was parked. She entered the doorway of a shop and peeked a look at the road. Ware could not be seen. It was only about fifty meters to her car, but she found she could not move towards it. It was fully fifteen minutes until she took the plunge. Darting out from the doorway, head grouched low and her top half covered by the umbrella she reached her car and had a quick look around. Seeing it was all clear, she started the engine and pulled out of the parking lot and headed to Inverness. Ware was in a restaurant when she set off. While planning, he finished his lunch and felt tired after the non-stop trip from Glasgow on his Harley. He decided to stay the night and head up to this Lochinver place he had heard Liz and Stuart often talk about tomorrow sharpish. With any luck he would find the bitch in a lonely Highland spot and put an end to it all. He booked into the Ferry Boat Inn, had a long bath and headed out to find a bar. At the same time Liz was passing Beauly and Morris and co were out for a walk along Lochinver front having booked into the Culag hotel and unpacked.

Despite the case in hand, Morris had found his thoughts consumed with his ex-girlfriend, Linda being in the location he had first met her and then years later started a relationship with her. He and Linda had split up a year ago. The cause, his infantile jealousy and lack of self-confidence. He accepted that grudgingly – it had been with him as a boy and followed him as he got older and had relationships. That he couldn't change. What he had not anticipated was that Linda would be walking around his head day after day, always wearing the same cream trousers and black sweater. In this relentless image she looked straight ahead and would suddenly turn to him with a weary, curt, smile, as if challenging him. This image jumped at Morris at any given time of the day out of nowhere and in his dreams all the time. He still loved her, he knew, but could he forgive? It was not a comfortable feeling he was experiencing. It was a mixture of longing and dread. He knew any meeting, or indeed any call, would be extremely uncomfortable heightened by the expected rejection. A part of him, a good part, was pushing him to just forget the whole thing. Then he would chastise himself for his cowardice and determine to call her, only for the doubts to return moments later. As they walked along the road towards the bridge, he noticed his son had been looking at him several times. As they reached the war memorial they stopped briefly to look at the names. Kevin turned to his father and said simply. 'Call her dad. You need to know one way or the other.' Morris smiled, loving his boy's quietness but succinctness yet again. He gulped involuntarily. 'Tonight' he determined, '...and the doubters can piss off.'

At six pm Morris came out the shower dried himself and prepared himself for the big call. He was as nervous as he had could recall. 'Considering what I have gone through, that's ridiculous!' he tried to laugh, failing miserably. He had decided on the location. Hotel room. Quiet. No interruptions- distractions. The time about six. Linda was always home then. If she went out it was about 8pm, so she would not be getting ready yet if she was 'Planning good, now pick up the phone you idiot. Be a man...God not that old adage again. I'm doing it, I'm doing it. Ok..' He picked up his mobile found her number far down the list and pressed call before he could change his mind. 'It's like I'm waiting to hear if I have cancer or not, for fucks sake...'

She answered.

'Hi Lochinver 247…'

'Linda. Hello. Its Sam here. I'm in Lochinver and thought I'd call and say hello…are you busy?'

'Sam. Hello there. Well it's a surprise for sure, though I knew you were here of course. And no, I am not busy.' She laughed slightly.

'You knew I was here?' Morris asked.

'It's Lochinver remember, we know everything,' Linda replied. There was some warmth there, Morris felt, encouraged by the offer.

'Linda…yes, we got here in the morning. Feels a bit strange to be here again, but nice. I'm with Kevin and a friend, Stuart Hislop.

'And you didn't phone me immediately?' she said, but the tone was sarcastic and humorous. 'Kevin is with you. I hadn't heard that though. I'd love to see him again. How long are you here for? Please tell him to drop by…if he wants to, of course.'

'Yes, he has said he would like to see you too. Not sure how long, maybe two or three days. Linda…'

She cut him off. 'Ok. Please ask him to come round for dinner tomorrow if he is free. We can talk about his lousy Dad all night.' But it was said without much malice. More, as Morris interpreted it optimistically, 'You are an idiot Sam and I'm acknowledging that, but maybe we can discuss this and take it from there.'

'Listen Linda…'

'Whheesh,' she interrupted. 'Just tell Kevin to come tomorrow and we will see after…'

'Thanks Linda, but I really want to say now, I'm so sorry.'

'Ok, Ok. Leave it please, Too quick. You can bring him to the door if you want. That ok?'

'More than ok. Thanks Linda. Eight ok?'

'Aye fine. Right Sam. Keep well. Bye….'

With that it was over. Morris felt a leaping of the spirit, as let out a long breath.

Morris woke up the next morning feeling good and refreshed. Kevin still lay immobile on the other bed. Stuart had his own room next door. The three of them had had a pleasant dinner the night before and a couple of Malts around the fireplace before retreating around 10 pm. Stuart had asked several people he knew if they had seen Liz recently, but there had been no positive response, though plenty of concerned questions about her wellbeing. Here, like everywhere else, she was a popular and respected friend. The concern was genuine.

Once everyone was up, they had a coffee and discussed their plans. Hislop was keen to try further north as he and Liz had often travelled to Drumbeg post Lochnver. Morris gave him an update on Linda feeling a bit awkward while doing so.

'…. ok, head up there, but I need to stay here a bit- tonight at least- Linda thing. Would you mind going up to Drumbeg yourself first? You going to stay there? '

'Will do, ok. Yes. I'll stay at a wee caravan in Nedd that we have stayed at, provided its available. I'll ask and see if she has been seen passing through or even staying. I think it's all a bit futile, but what else can we do? I wish she would just contact me and say something, damn it. What has happened to her…? It's frustrating, especially being here without her.'

'Right then,' said Morris. 'You head off and if things don't work out here I'll give you a call and you can pick us up and we will figure what to do next. Kevin fancies a walk up to Suilven, so could you drop us off at Kirkaig first?

'Aye, no bother,' replied Hislop. 'Ok, let's get moving. You want your walk and Kevin has a dinner date tonight, so better get going.' He winked at Kevin. 'Got enough Old Spice?' remembering Morris' favourite after shave.

They arrived at Inverkirkaig at noon. A walk up and back would take five or six hours and then back to the hotel to spruce up, Morris had calculated. It was a glorious day, nippy, but clear blue skies overhead. Morris recalled the summer of 1976 and basking in the sun in this magnificent landscape. About an hour into their walk they stopped for a rest and drink. They stopped and listened. It was one of these perfectly still moments which invited you to stop and muse. He looked around. There was no motion anywhere in their view which covered numerous square miles. He homed in on some heather and peered at it in challenge to move an iota. It remained totally motionless. Morris stared and took in its still beauty.

He tuned to the sky. Not a solitary cloud to be seen. 'Wordsmith, where are you?' he smiled. Almost hearing his own thought.

In the distance they could just see the sea behind. Enard bay was flat blue. He could not discern a ripple or a swirl. Not even a seagull darted through the sky. Just stillness everywhere. 'How often do you experience this in your life?' he thought, basking in it all. 'It's like another bloody planet.'

He sat down slowly on a bank by the path, subconsciously making as little noise as he could. He determined to wait in stillness himself until nature stirred into life again. Kevin was similarly caught up in the moment, looking around silently in wonder. Morris looked at Suilven above. 'The King of all your surrounds. How you like it I'm sure,' he thought 'Still, unmoving, serene – like yourself'. A moment later the first sound came. It sounded like a splash. He turned from Suilven and looked instinctively towards the sea. From their high vantage point more than a mile way he could make out a small boy in shorts throwing large stones into the water down at

Inverkirkaig. Morris would see the splash and a few seconds later the sound would reach him. He could not resist. Standing up, he hollowed out his palms at the side of his face and shouted. 'Hello'. The sound boomed out in all directions. Hitting of rocks and barren hills. A few seconds later the wee boy who had been reaching down for more ammunition glanced around in shock. Morris laughed, stood up straight and waved frantically. The boy in turn searched wildly amongst the road near the beach and then raising his view upwards eventually saw Morris and Kevin as small points in the distance and waved back. Two specks in the silent landscape. 'McCaig, you should have been here today,' Morris smiled, remembering his fathers' poet friend who visited and wrote poems about Assynt. Kevin meanwhile had had a pee on a rock. Morris could not resist.

'Kevin Morris. The first man to pee on that rock for a billion years. How does it feel son?'

Kevin looked down at his trickle on the Torridonian Sandstone. 'It's an honour to be the first,' he laughed. He looked up at Suilven and asked Morris. 'Suilven. Any idea what it means Dad?'

'I do indeed. It's a mixture of the Norse 'Sula' meaning pillar and 'Beinn'- Gaelic for mountain. Can you imagine the Vikings coming through the Minch and seeing it for the first time? Exactly the same as we are seeing now tens of hundreds of years ago…' He stared at the mountain and then the sea in wonderment, then turned back to his son. He shook his head and stood up quickly.

'Ok, enough of the aesthetics. Looking forward to the meal tonight Kev?'

Kevin nodded. 'You coming at all?'

'Just to the gate, but maybe after…'

'You blew it with her Dad you know.' Kevin said with a hint of disappointment.

'I sure did,' Morris replied with a grimace. 'Lesson learnt- appreciate what you have. This is bloody magnificent isn't it? The silence, the view…' They looked around once more, soaking it all up and turned back to the looming mountain ahead of them. They reached Suilven two hours later, stayed half an hour and then headed back directly to Lochinver by passing Inverkirkaig going directly over the hills to ensure a shorter walk back. They got to the Culag hotel at five thirty. By six thirty they were both ready for the night. Kevin stayed in his room ensconced in Facebook, while Morris headed down to Wayfarers bar. The bar was empty save for one old man sitting next to the fireplace. Morris remembered him from years before though they had never talked. He wasn't the talking type. He failed to look up as Morris approached the bar as he searched to warm his soul and find answers within the dancing flames. Morris recalled his many sessions in the pub with Jon Cain, his best pal, who had had a house in Lochinver. He had passed away peacefully a year ago and his wife Magda had sold up and returned to Indonesia where she still had some family. Morris ordered a pint and sat at a bar stool. He contemplated times past as he sipped, his mind never far from Linda. Two years ago he had been reunited with her after years without seeing her and it was in in this very bar. He remembered their eyes meeting across the bar and the excitement that had been sparked by it. After the Tosa case and his retirement, he had moved up here with her and then it all went wrong after only two months. They had split up and he had moved back to Glasgow. He caught the noise of the bar door opening and instinctively turned his head. He couldn't believe it. In the doorway stood William Ware who had popped his head through and was looking around. Their eyes met and held for a second. There was a brief hesitation on Ware's face, a very slight movement backwards, and then he shook his head, smiled and strode towards Morris.

'Sam Morris.' He reached out his hand which Morris shook. 'Hells bells. A small world indeed and tiny up here I know. Are you on holiday?'

Morris' head was jumping with possibilities. He would contact Stuart later and decided to not mention Hislop's whereabouts for the moment.

'Sort of. And yourself?' Again the tiniest hesitation crossed Ware's face, but he too was thinking rapidly.

'Same for me,' Ware replied. 'A wee break. Got five days free. Stuart often talked about the Highlands, so thought I'd give it a go. Wish I had come before. Magnificent. I drove up on my bike. Straight to Ullapool. Night there and then I'll have a day, or two here. You by yourself?'

'Just with my son. He is up in his room and then he is going out to dinner later.'

'Good stuff. Looks a nice hotel if a bit pricey. Bugger it. I'll treat myself for one night at least. Drink first though. A pint?'

Morris eyed him closely, but thanked him as Ware sat down next to him and looked around. 'Nice pub,' he said. 'That old guy in the corner looks like he lives here. Away with the fairies, or some other heavenly body…'

'I remember him from way back,' Morris mentioned. 'He was much the same then. He survived a boat sinking in the Minch. He was in the water fifteen minutes when they hauled him out. The rest of the crew all died, including two seventeen year olds from Bucky. Now he just sits by the fire and looks into it most of the night.'

'Phew. Some story. Poor fucker,' Ware said staring at the old man for a second. He ordered a pint for him which the bar tender took over. The old man took the pint, turned to Ware and Morris, nodded and reentered the portal into his own place somewhere distant and past. His eyes - reflecting the fire - still somehow looked cold.

Ware continued. 'I called Stuart to see if he wanted to have a trip somewhere and thought maybe he fancied a break, but he said it looked like he had to go to London for a seminar or something. Then I thought about the Highlands and on a spur of the moment packed my bags, jumped on the bike and off I went. Great decision... Have you seen Stuart yourself since we met? How is he doing?'

'A couple of times,' replied Morris, still, wary, still judging the situation.

'Ah - and what about his wife,' said Ware, looking into his pint and taking a decent swig. Still nothing?'

'No,' Morris only said, noting that Ware had diverted his eyes from him as he spoke.

'Ach, she'll turn up. Just a wee tiff between them for being ignored. Mind you, she was bang out of order with that other guy. Phew, bad one.'

'Yes, you said that before. Well let's hope it's all resolved amicably.' replied Morris. He was wary, but this was a further chance to learn more about Ware, Anne, Hislop and his wife. He decided to gamble.

'You know Anne Smith; I think?'

'Anne Smith? Of course. Stuart, Ian and I were best pals and we used to meet up sometimes with the girls for a curry. Awful news about his death. Just crossing the road and that's it. You think the driver would have handed themselves in, out of decency. Some people are just cunts though.'

'Again the language. It doesn't fit.' Morris thought.

'I must contact Anne and see how she is doing.' Ware added.'I saw her at the funeral and she looked in a pretty bad way. Between you and me,' he said, leaning closer to Morris, 'she has a bit of a drink problem.'

Morris thought of that night he had taken Anne home. She had polished off a bottle of wine in less than twenty minutes and then, after throwing up in the lounge, she had been sick all night. Once he had to wake her up to throw up as he could see she was about to despite being asleep. If he hadn't been there god knows what could have happened. He had felt loathe to leave her till she eventually stirred at about six am. Yes, she had a problem alright.

Kevin Morris approached Liz's front door looking as presentable as he could and carrying six cans of beer and a bottle of wine. Morris hovered at the gate shifting nervously. Ware had decided to book into the hotel where they had had a drink and they had said they would meet up in the morning. On getting back to his room to pick up his son, Morris had phoned Hislop and told him that Ware was in Lochinver and what he had said. He seemed embarrassed.

'Shit. I didn't feel good lying to him about my whereabouts. He's my oldest pal remember. But if you think its best… Ok. If he calls, I'll say I'm still down south. How long is he here for, any idea?'

'Just a day, or two, I think. He is booked into the same Hotel as us. Look, it's been a nice wee break, but we haven't really found anything to suggest that Liz was here, so I guess we should head back to Glasgow soon and take it from there. Or do you think otherwise?' Morris said.

'I'm thinking the same. Maybe it was a bit daft to think that she would go somewhere I knew about but remembering her character, I thought she would go somewhere she knew, but she considered isolated and safe. Wrong, looks like. I asked around here too. Nothing. You just want to head back tomorrow?'

Morris hesitated. 'Could do. It's just that I have been in contact with Linda and well… I would like to spend some time with her if that proves to be a possibility. Maybe you could go back with Kevin and I'll get the train down later? I'll know more after tonight I think. Kevin is going for dinner at her place and I'll see how the lay of the land is. So you staying there tonight again and I'll call in the morning. That ok?'

'Aye, that's fine,' said Hislop. 'Speak to you then and good luck…'

Liz answered the door soon after Kevin had knocked. She gave Kevin a cuddle which he embraced warmly and gestured towards the hallway. 'Come in, come in. My word, a full man now. Wine for me?' She pecked Kevin on the cheek and he went in towards the sitting room. 'I'll be with you in a minute,' she said to him, turning towards Morris who stood motionless at the gate.

He waved to her, despite Linda being only about five meters away.

'Linda. Hi. Thanks so much for the invitation. Kev has been looking forward to it all day.'

'It's my pleasure. Thanks for the wine. You remembered my favourite.'

'Mais Oui' Morris said and they both laughed.

There was a pause as their eyes caught.

Morris gulped. 'Linda. I don't have time, so will just say it. I'm sorry for everything. I got it badly wrong. I don't know why. Insecure I guess. Anyway, just to say…'

They stared at each other intently. Eventually she spoke.

'I won't pretend that you did not hurt me. It was mostly the fact that you could not trust me which hurt. I thought you knew that I would never…' she said.

'I know, I know. I feel like a fool. Worse than that…' Morris said.

She stared hard at him again - obviously coming to some conclusion.

'…Ok. After Kevin has finished his dinner come back and we will have a chat. Better bring another bottle of wine too.'

'Tell Kevin he has ten minutes', said Morris and they laughed together as they used to.

'Thank you,' he added. 'Give us a call please when you are done. I'll go and get the wine and wait in my room. And thanks again.'

She smiled and shut the door. Kevin, who had been listening near the door smiled too as he poured his first beer and unscrewed the wine. He wouldn't keep his Dad too long he smiled to himself.

When you fear the worst and instead get good news there is no feeling like it, Morris concluded as he strode towards the off license. Was there a special word for it? 'Relief?' Totally insufficient. It wasn't just that he had navigated a potentially awkward situation with apparent success it was the aftermath. The warm glow, the heightened senses, that wonderful feeling that all was good in the world. He saw a seagull perched on the slate roof of a house and found himself asking it if it would like salt and vinegar with its Fish and Chips. It seemed to nod as it gave a brief screech. Everything was great, all was good in the world for now. Sure he was anxious about later, but he would be near her again, that's all that mattered and he was not going to blow it …

While Morris was walking light of foot back to the hotel, in Drumbeg, Stuart Hislop had just booked into the caravan in Nedd for a further night and gone for a walk over the hills towards Loch Poli. There was a fresh cool wind which seemed to whisper thoughts in his ear as he thought again of Liz. God, how he loved her he realised yet again. But he thought soberly, maybe it was time to give it a rest. It must be that she had just had enough and decided to take a break, or even a fresh start. That would account for her not even contacting Anne, her best pal. Her behaviour was strange indeed, but Hislop was sure that it would not be the first time a woman (or man) had decided a sudden and total changing of the guard was the only solution to perceived problems. Was she in danger? Or worried about something? That seemed unlikely. From and about what? But he would so like to just know that she was fine. 'How very little we really know someone', he concluded. 'Oh, we think we do alright, but we only see how they act in their moments with other humans. What really goes on inside someone's head we will never know and no one ever really tells it all'. He stopped walking, stopped for a minute as he looked over Loch Poli. He shrugged involuntarily as he drifted back to the real world and turned back towards the caravan. About half a mile away from it, and on the road behind it, he saw that someone was waving to him. A man. About his age looked like, but he did not recognize him. The man finished waving and stood waiting for Hislop to approach. As he got near, Hislop saw it was Lewis Macaskill an old friend of his and Liz's. Not a man from Drumbeg though.

Inverkirkaig. Hislop waved back as he got near and shouted.

'Lewis MacAskill. How are you doing? There's a surprise…'

'Thought it was you,' replied Lewis. 'Heard today that you were in the hotel with Sam Morris and his son. I'm just heading back after a delivery here; you need a lift or anything?'

'No. I'm staying here for a couple of days, in the caravan there.'

MacAskill looked at it in confusion.

'Here? What for. The Hotel? And the others? And your wife in Inverkirkaig. Totally confused man.'

'Liz?' Morris stammered.

'That's her name- glad you remember it.' MacAskill smiled. 'In a caravan at Badnaban. Didn't you know?' Suddenly he looked extremely embarrassed and looked away.

'No, no, it's alright. I can explain, but she is here. She is fine? You actually saw her?' Hislop said.

'I did indeed unless it was an aberration?' MacAskill laughed again. 'Don't know what the hell is going on here, but she is there. I saw her walking along the beach and back. Fine as far as I know. Greta McLeod lets the caravan out. Lochinver 270, if you need the number.'

'Yes!' said Hislop, punching the air. 'Lewis…sorry, it's a long story. I'll tell you the basics. Liz left me suddenly without any real reason. I was a bit worried and she contacted no one, so with Sam, thought we would try and find her. Up here looked a logical place. Quiet and secluded. I forgot about that caravan though. We walked past it many a time. Should have thought it was a possible hiding place.'

'Seems a bit drastic trying to locate her. Just give her time, if you don't mind me saying…'

'I know, but the circumstances of her suddenly leaving and especially the non-contact were worrying. I even thought she might be dead at first. I'd just like to talk to her, see if she is alright and I guess if she wants to be a hermit that's up to her, but would be tough… she did call another friend very briefly and apparently sounded worried, so that didn't help us relax, though at least it showed she was alive.'

MacAskill stared. 'What? Dead? Did you think she had been murdered or something?'

'No, it's hard to explain. Just there was a need to know feeling?'

'Ok… understand. Anyway, glad I can help. So head down there tomorrow and reunite with her. Hope it all goes well. I must get back. Dinner in half an hour.' They shook hands and MacAskill headed off to car giving Hislop one last bewildered look as he did so.

Hislop phoned Morris immediately.

'Found her!' he exclaimed. 'She is here- up at Inverkirkaig. Staying in a caravan just up the road in

Badnaban. I have the owners number; I'll call her now and check Liz is still there.'

'No don't.' Morris said firmly. 'The owner would be bound to tell Liz and Liz had probably told her if anyone asks about her to tell her. She might just bugger off before you get a chance to talk things out with her. Just go up there in the morning and chat with her. Well! This is great news. So we were right to come up here after all. Things looking good all round. We will chat in the in the morning and sort it all out. Now you must excuse me pal. I may have a hot date tonight.' They finished the call. Fifteen minutes later Morris got the anticipated call from Linda.

'That was a bit quicker than I thought it would be,' he said down the phone. 'Once Kevin gets chatting there is normally no stopping him.'

'We had a lovely chat, but I had other things on my mind.' She replied with a tiny hint of seduction. 'See you soon…' 'Jesus Christ,' Morris muttered to himself and smiled as he left the room and practically jumped down the stairs. He passed the bar then thought he had better check on Ware in case he could not meet up with him in the morning. He went back, popped his head in the doorway and saw that Ware was still there. Ware did not notice him and by his splattered hair and gesticulations was obviously well gone with the drink. Ware sat with three teenage boys who looked slightly shell shocked. Empty pints were all over the small table and half-drunk nips too. Morris decided that Ware would not be in any fit state in the morning. He turned to go. He gave a last look to check he had not been seen. Ware was showing the company something on his phone. As he did so he saw him reach across the table and place his hand briefly on one of the boy's knees who shifted away nervously. 'Bloody hell,' thought Morris. 'That was a move.' He left the bar unnoticed. He bounced around a few ideas in his head, these were soon quelled by thoughts of meeting Linda and the time that lay ahead. Walking along Lochinver front towards her place he noticed Kevin striding towards him. They stopped for a chat and Morris informed him that they had located Liz and Hislop would go and talk to her in the morning. Depending on the outcome of that, they would possibly be heading back to Glasgow in the afternoon.

'Unless you fancy staying a few days' here?'

Kevin smiled. 'That's fine with me Dad. Could this be related to you and Linda per wild chance? 'He laughed out loud. He was happy, Morris could see in his smile, his gait and his eyes.

'Subtlety was never my strong point.' Morris laughed.' Ok, see you back in the room…some time later.'

He felt relaxed as he knocked on Linda's door. Elated almost. In the darkest times he believed he would never see her again, but here he was about to be with her. He knew though that first something had to be broached.

She answered the door quickly and ushered him in to the living room. She took the bottle of wine from him and returning from the kitchen with two glasses poured two half full.

As she sat down next to him on the sofa, he quickly spoke.

'Linda. I think we have to…I mean I have to clear the air here. I hope it does not spoil anything. First, you were right to ask me to leave. I was a bloody idiot. Look, you know my background, just when I saw you kiss Alistair, I lost it in petty jealousy. I should never have spoken to you like that. I don't know, something from when I was young. I got jealous and worse…it all boiled over. You know I'm not normally like that. We were all drunk, it was no big deal…'

She stared at him intently for a minute, then spoke.

'You are wrong. It was a big deal. I used to go out with him and had not seen him in years and I just sort of forgot and kissed him for a minute. Why, I don't really know. I didn't miss him, or anything and nothing was going to come off it, but to do that in front of your face…no, not right. You had been talking to Dezzy so maybe I was a wee bit jealous too. To be honest I was out of it and can't remember much. I'm sorry for all that, but what you called me was over the top and my pride, or maybe defense mechanisms kicked in…'

It was a charged atmosphere. Two people wanting to be near each other, but wary and fearful of ruining the prospects by a false move, or word. Nevertheless, without realising it they had inched closer to each other and now were just a foot away. Saying nothing, Morris raised his hand slowly and reached towards her cheek. He stopped for a second and then stroked her face gently. Linda let out a slow breath of air, closed her eyes and tilted her head to the side. The mutual fear of rejection dissipated as they willingly moved together. They slid onto the thick orange carpet beneath the sofa…

Afterwards they lay next to each other, bathing in the glorious aftermath of their shared longings and warmth for each other. Presently, he raised himself and moved over her. 'More wine Madam?' he said smiling intoning a phony French accent.

'Certainly garcon. But please do something for me first?'

'And what might that be Madam?' Morris asked in mocking servitude.

'Kindly wash your face- one side of it is covered in orange carpet shreds.'

Later that night they talked at length and Linda agreed to move down to Glasgow at the end of the month. She needed to hand in and work her notice and sell her flat. Morris gave her the basics behind the search for Liz and asked for her opinion.

'From what you say about the way your friend was treating her, I'm not surprised she left. As for not telling him, that would be to give him a shock and she would think that would make him come to his senses. If she had planned to run off with that guy she shagged in the house, she would have told him, because the whole thing would have been finished and there would be a lot to sort out. To me she obviously wanted to stay with your friend, Stuart was it, and thought some dramatics might help. Unless something else was going on that you didn't tell me.'

Morris nodded. 'That could be it. Well she is here and Stuart will see her in a few hours. It would be nice if they could sort it out like we did,' he smiled. He grabbed her waist and they entwined again.

Later Morris walked back to the Hotel as the sun came up. He felt weightless in mind and body as he ambled along stopping frequently to look around. The sea was calm and seagull cries echoed around the harbor. Morris thought how wonderful the world could really be in its finest moments such as then.

Stuart Hislop got up before six, not having slept well. He packed up, paid his bill and phoned Morris just before getting into the car. No answer. 'Lucky bastard', he thought. He decided to drive to the Hotel in Lochinver. He did and went up to the room. Kevin answered the knock and peering in the room he could see Morris stirring slowly.

'Sorry to bother you lover boy, but I'm just heading up for a rendezvous of my own. Bloody hell, what happened to your face- one side of it is all orange? He winked at Kevin and they both laughed. Morris rubbed his eyes, slowly coming round, then getting out of bed.

'Ok. Got it. Sorry, sorry. Late night... Ok, so you will head up to have it out with Liz. That's great. Hopefully you can sort it all out. Be conciliatory and sympathetic for goodness sake though. We will wait for you here and we will see what to do next. And no more face comments you two,' he laughed, peering into the mirror with a mock grimace. The mood of them all was decidedly light. Things were going well.

'Right see you back here. I'm off,' Hislop said quickly and shut the door. He drove the two and a half miles to Inverkirkcaig in anticipatory excitement. On getting there he saw the sign saying Badnaban and turned off to the right. He soon a caravan ahead. An old lady was outside one of them. He stopped the car and got out. 'Hello. Good morning. How are you? My name is Stuart Hislop and my wife is staying here.'

The lady looked at him and raised her eyebrows. 'Hislop? No one called Hislop was here. Just one caravan let out here this week. To a lady called Harris. Never said Hislop, I'm sure. She left yesterday morning. Before her booking was finished actually. Nice lady.'

Hislop felt his heart sink. He opened his phone and displayed a photo of his wife. The old lady looked closely and nodded and then frowned. 'Hislop you said? Sure she said Harris.' She was already looking forward to telling the gossip to her friends. 'As I said, she left yesterday. She was in a hired car if that helps. Did you have a fight or something?'

'No, well yes, sort of.' Hislop said. 'Look, how was she- did she look ok?'

'Aye, she was fine. Kept much to herself though. I saw her talking a few walks along the front, but apart from that barely saw her. She said little, just paid in advance and left early. She looked a wee bit sad when I saw her walking.'

Hislop nodded, thanked Greta McLeod and got back into his car. He banged the car wheel, 'Bastards', he called out in utter frustration.

He returned to Lochinver and the Culag Hotel and saw Morris and Kevin in the dining room, just finishing off breakfast. They talked about what to do. Hislop was fed up and just wanted to get back to Glasgow. Kevin was keen too, having got a call from a pal who wanted to meet up there. Morris wanted to stay a few days to see Linda, but decided to discuss it with her first. He called Linda, then went over to her place before she started work. She agreed that he should get down the road and confirmed she was handing in her notice that day and would be down in Glasgow at the end of the month and putting her place up for sale. There was a comfortable feeling between them. A barrier had been overcome and for now, all looked good. Morris kissed her lightly and headed for the door. It took him an hour to reach it, but he enjoyed the journey immensely.

CHAPTER 7

It was a fine night in Glasgow (so far) and the Doublet was busier than normal. Gary Scott sat at the bar as was his wont preferring a wee chat with many as they came to get a drink to a specific few if he sat at the tables. Earlier he had seen his daughter and grandson who had come round for lunch, so he felt content and in good spirits. Then Phil Burns aka 'The Philosopher' walked in looking keenly around. 'Jesus t'fuck', Scott murmured to himself, grabbing his newspaper and peering at it intently. The trouble was that Phil was quite a nice guy. Postman and musician. He just brought all his conspiracy theories and musings into the pub to share with anyone who would listen and there was always one who he would be able to home in on. While diving into his paper Scott wondered about conspiracy theorists. Once you even remotely accepted the possibility that Hitler was still hosting tea parties in Buenos Aries, or that Elvis was living quietly in the Rocky Mountains, anything at all – any person, any subject- could be manipulated to meet your own suspicious and paranoia. Scott shrugged slightly. Human nature to be suspicious and extrapolate to cover all possibilities. It's one of the reasons we survived. 'Fine, fine,' Scott argued with himself, 'But it's hard to see how believing the landing on the moon was actually shot in a backwater studio in Holywood advances the cause of Human progression.' Scott laughed to himself as he realised that even seeing Phil had got him thinking about things.

'Captain Birds Eye! The man with the Golden Fish fingers! How you doing?' The Philosopher had spoken, obviously to him. 'Shite,' Scott thought and then suddenly had an idea. 'Two can play at that game…'

Looking from his paper he stated in somber tone.

'It depends on what you mean'. He had hoped this would throw Burns off course, or at least remind him of the type of statements that he himself often came out with, thus, hopefully, leading to a reconsideration of how he approached pub banter. No chance of that…

'That's remarkable Gary.' Burns said nodding profusely. 'Most people just say 'good' fine' or 'awright' but you are right, it's never as easy as that.' How glib to simply state, 'I'm fine'. I was thinking that the other day. Totally meaningless actually. Anyways, so things not going so good?'

Scott was trapped already. 'What to do? May as well indulge....'

'Well, I'm fine (deliberately raising his hands and doing the quotation signal for the first time in his life). But I have been thinking a lot recently.'

'Me too,' Burns replied. 'I find it helps. Thinking is good for the brain. By the way Fish Fingers is good for that.'

'Aye, right,' replied Scott. 'Well, I started to think about my life. It just seems to have passed me by without any real meaning. Its nearly over and what have I done that will leave a mark. I don't know, feel useless and a failure.'

'A lot of people feel like that when they get older, I know. I have talked to many in pubs and around. I'm a bit younger, but get that too sometimes. You know, there was a song by Nat King Cole that used to help me when I was down.'

'And what was that?' Scott could not help himself asking.

Rather than say the words, Burns looked around the bar, fixed his gaze at the gantry and started to hum a tune. After a few bars he sang.

'Pick yourself up, dust yourself down and start all over again. Work like a soul inspired till the battle of the day is won. You may be sick and tired, but you will be a man my son.' Andrew the barman raised his eyebrows and glanced at Burns momentarily, but continued to clean the glass he was holding. Phil took a large swig of his pint and added. 'I think that last bit says it all. Life is a bitch, but you have to keep going. Be a man my son. Great.'

'Christ o' Mighty,' Scott thought. 'He's singing Philosophical songs by well-known philosphical contemplator Nat King Cole at five thirty in the evening. Me thinks you have been doing quite a bit of philosophising around the pubs already today,' Scott found himself inwardly laughing.

'So if life is a bitch and then you are dead, what's the bloody point of it all, apart from keep getting up and trying again,' declared Scott, now getting caught in the thread and looking down at his pint solemnly.

'I find it best to just remember we are Monkeys.' Smith said.

'Monkeys...?' Scott had been ready for most answers, but that one threw him a bit.

'Yes, Monkeys, or Minkeys if you are Peter Sellers' Burns laughed a bit too loudly. A few of the regulars on the tables glanced over, but seeing who it was soon returned to their conversations.

'Still do not know what you mean exactly?' Scott asked becoming interested despite himself.

'Monkeys, apes. That's where we came from six million years ago. Think it was a Saturday night,' he laughed again, receiving further withering looks from the pub patrons. Andrew, the barman, pushed his head forward, raised his eyebrows, put his middle finger to his lips and tried to catch the attention of Burns.

'Aye, I know that it was millions of years ago… so?' Scott replied after acknowledging the joke with a small and much quieter laugh himself.

'Well that's it,' Burns declared spreading his arms. 'All human behavior can be traced back to Monkey genes and instincts if you think about it. Not just hunger and thirst, but you see in monkey societies the need for a hierarchy of power- we have the same. Another thing. Why do men get jealous of women for example? Why should it matter is she is flirting or even shagging some other guy as long as he gets his share?'

'Not sure… it doesn't seem right that's all…' Scott replied.

'Aye but why? I'll tell you why. Because the guy need his sperm to get her pregnant and if she is with or even attracted to another his wee tadpoles might not be the ones that do the trick. And…he would never know. You see. Jealousy explained. Monkeys…'

'Ah,' said Scott defiantly. 'Women get jealous too, so what about that?'

'Monkeys again…' said Burns immediately.

Scott frowned. 'What do you mean Monkeys again?'. 'Glasgow on a Tuesday evening,' he thought. 'You never can tell, or predict what the hell you will end up talking about. That was the beauty of the place.'

Burns was now in full flow. 'Right, Same thing. Women can get pregnant by any guy – true - but she needs a man to stay around long enough to help bring up her child, so obviously if he is looking around at others that's a threat. Voila. Jealousy again. After the kid is about seven she doesn't need the guy so much, so she might choose another one for the next child. Seven-year itch. Heard of that? Monkeys are the same. So if you are down, or depressed, or jealous it is good to know where it came from and at least you understand that its natural-and it's from the Monkeys. Then you can dust yourself down and start all over again as the man with the velvet voice said.' Burns concluded, took a very large gulp of beer and looked around the bar as if expecting a round of applause. None was forthcoming.

'That's food for thought' said Scott thinking of bananas, nuts, PG Tips and King Kong as he spoke. 'You know you should have been a psychiatrist. I think if everyone knew about these Monkey instincts it could help them. No need for pills and other stuff…'

The hint of sarcasm was missed by Burns

'Quite a few people have said that to me. I think it's too late now though. Anyway, I like being a postman. Gives me time to think about things.'

'Keep thinking Batman,' Scott replied with a smile. 'Let me buy you a pint before I go. That was an interesting chat.'

'Ah, you have to go – thanks for the pint- I was just getting going.'

'I know - that's why I'm fucking off.' Scott whispered to himself and then chastising himself immediately. 'He's alright, actually that was a decent wee chat…Monkeys.'

Scott arrived home half an hour later. He looked in the fridge for a dinner decision. The pint he had bought Burns had meant he had gone over his budget for the day, so punishment was deserved. He took out six fish fingers from the pack of twelve in the freezer, then returned two and headed for the frying pan. That would have to suffice. He had moved the cooker next to the window from where he could look out to Kelvingrove park while cooking. He liked that. He was staring at a young couple and a dog as they entered the park when it came to him suddenly. The women in the car. 'Julia Sinclair!' She had worked in a travel agency on Byres road that he used to go to. He always chose the same shop and the same assistant, Julia. They had got along well. He was sure she was even flirting with him. Once when he had booked a holiday to Zakinthos she had said how she would love to go there and the way she let it linger, he jumped to the hopeful conclusion that she might want to actually go with him, but he had been too feart to pursue it. She was a looker for sure. How had he forgotten her until now? While he had summoned up the considerable courage (for him) to ask her if she might possibly join him for a meal, or failing that a two-week holiday in Greece (separate beds, of course), he had gone into the shop one day and saw her with her partner as they cuddled and kissed before she sat down again after her lunchtime break. Scott remembered the feeling now that had consumed him then. Jealousy. Monkey jealousy. But maybe she was free now after all these years he now thought. She had still looked great in the car even though it looked like something had frightened her. As he turned over his four fish fingers he determined to try and find Julia Sinclair.

Colin Shaw was in a meeting but he was finding it hard to concentrate. It was the same feeling that he had felt it seemed every minute since Julia had told him about the Hit and Run. Dread and uncertainty. He had told her immediately not to go to the police. She had protested but he had made it very clear. They would ask her questions and why had she not stopped could lead to the discovery of their affair and that just could not be allowed to happen. If she told them where she had been and with who they would want to talk with him to verify. If the press got a hold of it… Worst of all, his kids who loved their mother, would never speak to him again. Of that he was sure. Of course, he was reassuring when Julia phoned which was regularly. But they had dared not meet since the accident and he felt a growing tension between them. He had made it clear, but as non-aggressively as possible that she could not go to the police. She had sold the car as he had instructed, which was good. He had told her that they just had to wait till it all blew over to meet again but the last time she had phoned she had started to cry and saying he was trying to dump her. Actually she was spot on, but he dared not tell her in case she went to the police in retribution. The meeting finished. It was a brewery takeover bid that he had been planning for over a year. His biggest deal yet. He would let nothing destroy it. When he got back to his office he slumped into his chair. The phone went. He answered. It was his daughter. He adored her and his son. Thinking about them, just made him more determined to end the relationship with Julia. After the call he went over to the Cabinet and poured himself a malt added a single ice cube and went over to the couch near the window overlooking George square. It was a good life he had built for himself and he had much to lose. As he basked the phone went again. It was her. Somehow he had known it would be.

'Hello Colin. Julia here. You ok? You haven't called in three days…'

'I'm sorry. Yes, I have been really busy with that company takeover thing I mentioned.'

'Colin. Listen. It's been weeks since the accident. Nothing is going to happen. I told no one and sold the car. Its fine, but you refuse to meet me. I need to see you.'

'I know it's been a long time, I feel it too, but you know my situation. Family and work. It's impossible to meet for a while longer.'

Perhaps he had said it wrong, but the reaction from Julia was not as he had expected.

'Don't take me for a bloody fool Colin. It's quite clear that your cherished reputation is all you care about. What an idiot I have been. You don't want to see me again do you?'

'Look, Julia. I...just wait a bit longer. Can't you understand?'

'I have waited and waited and nothing from you. I killed a man and you can't even say you love me anymore. I tell you what mister. We meet within a week or I go to the police like I should have done in the beginning. And I will make sure I will tell them exactly where I was that night.'

'Julia, wait.' Colin said desperately, his mind racing.

'No waiting. Up yours, I'll take you to the cleaners. And just remember I know plenty about you and your contacts and your sleaze, so just treat me right, you bastard, otherwise the papers might get an surprise call. You get the idea. Fifty thousand is the price. Just call me when its arranged. Goodbye.'

With that, the phone went dead. Shaw drained his drink and continued looking out over George square for fully ten minutes before deciding on what he believed necessary to solve his predicament. As he looked at some fluttering pigeons rising together towards the grey sky, he shrugged and smiled grimly. 'So be it', he muttered. 'So be it.' Life always presented difficult challenges that had to be overcome. He began to plan…who could he get to do the job? Ringo? Was he ready for a step up? Anyway, he didn't have time to try and find a professional. He muttered to himself, then made the call. Ringo had agreed to it after being told how much he would get for the job and they had haggled a bit. After it was arranged, Worth popped round to his bank in Sauchiehall street and withdrew twelve thousand pounds. He had offered twenty at first, but was glad to settle for twenty four- twelve up front and the rest after the job was done. He placed the envelope with the money in the top right pocket of his jacket and headed for the meet with Ringo. At the meeting in a quiet bar, he explained what had to be done. Ringo looked excited. Worth got the impression that Ringo was also chuffed to be trusted with such serious business. It would be done by tomorrow Worth had been assured. The money was exchanged and Julia's address passed on…

Gary Scott woke up with a plan already in his head. Dressing quickly, he headed up to Byres road. He stopped for a quick coffee and then entered the Travel Agency that he had used to go to and Julia

Sinclair had once worked- maybe still did so, though it was ten years ago since he had last had the money for a holiday and had not been in since he had moved back to Glasgow. He entered and walked as smartly as he could to a free counter. Looking around he saw no sign of Julia.

'Good morning,' he said to the young girl behind the counter. Some memories were immediately rekindled as he sat down. Much of the shop looked the same as before. A photo of Istanbul still there in the corner. 'I was wondering if you can help me with something.' He asked as politely as he could.

The well-dressed girl looked up and smiled. 'Thinking of a holiday sir?' She could have only been about twenty years old.

'Eh, actually no if you don't mind. I'll tell you. I used to come here often years ago and there was a lady I used to talk too and well, we sort of lost contact, I mean, we never had contact, but I was wondering if anyone knew her and maybe could pass on a message for me? Julia Sinclair… worked here before…'

The assistant listened intently but with some suspicion. Eventually she rose from her chair. 'Hold on a wee minute.' Scott realised he was blushing. He had started to wish he had never come. Stupid idea. His thoughts were interrupted by an approaching figure. He recognized her vaguely.

'Mr Scott isn't it? said the lady in front of him 'I'm Lorna, the Manager. I remember you from years ago. How are you doing? You stopped coming here what – ten, twelve years ago?'

'Yes, long time. I remember you too,' Scott said getting off his chair and accepting the offered hand. He laughed. 'Ran out of money for holidays when I stopped working. Amazing- you even remembered my name. Forgotten yours, sorry.'

'My job. Lorna Boyd. Now, Eileen says you are looking for Julia. May I ask why?'

Scott blushed. 'I'm sorry. It's just I was thinking of her yesterday and thought it would be nice to see her again after all these years. She has stopped working here I suppose?'

'Yes, about five years ago. We were sorry to see her go. Her husband died and she stopped soon after.'

'Oh, that's a shame,' Scott said, thinking the exact opposite as regards her husband. 'Look I know it sounds strange but do you have any contact number for her? I mean, not for me, but if you have, could you possibly ask her if she would like to maybe see me again for a wee catch up over a drink, or meal?'

Lorna Boyd smiled. 'Yes, I can do that for you. We are in contact often. No promises though,' she laughed. 'Give us your number and I'll give her a call later and pass it on.'

Scott gave his number, thanked the two ladies and left. 'Well, maybe there was a chance,' he thought none too hopefully.

He stocked up with another five packets of Fish fingers two tins of processed peas and a half kilo of mince at Iceland and headed home.

He enjoyed his later trip to the Doublet. The Philosopher was thankfully not in and he sat thinking about the day and Julia. He was proud that he had summoned up the courage to go into the shop and now he sat at home with his (own) fingers mentally crossed. He was just nodding off in front of the TV around ten when the phone went. He answered quickly. 'Is that Gary Scott there? This is Julia Sinclair…'

Gary Scott was taken aback by Julia's call. She had asked him soon enough why he had tried to contact her again after all these years.

'It was just a couple of unexpected events that made me think of you. I actually saw you in a car a few weeks ago, but didn't remember you at the time. You have a Blue Mercedes, yes?' he asked.

'Yes, that would have been me in the car. I sold it though- times are hard,' she laughed, but there was a slight edge to her words.

'Anyway, it was strange I was talking to a bloke in the pub yesterday, went home and suddenly remembered your name. I remembered that you used to work up in Byres road and just thought it would be nice to see how you were doing? Hope you don't mind. I heard about your husband. I'm sorry.' Scott said.

"Yes, Jack died five years ago. Not the same without him. It was nice having company…' she let that one drag for a few seconds. 'And yourself?'

'Still single. I think it's safe to say, that's it for me, but I would love to meet up and have a chat if you could possibly manage that. But… maybe you are with someone again?' he asked.

Julia Sinclair hesitated for a moment before answering. Should she tell him? No, she decided. Anyway very soon she would be free of Colin and considerably better off to boot. She smiled into the phone.

'It was such a lovely surprise to hear that you wanted to contact me again. I have been a little down lately, so it made my day Gary. I would love to meet you for a catch up and we will see how it goes. Would you like to come here for dinner tomorrow night? I make a nice Chicken A La King, if you fancy.'

'That would be wonderful Julia. I'll bring wine, or something else?'

'Just bring yourself and be prepared for lots of chat.' Julia had replied warmly, so pleased to indulge in mild flirting after her tensions with Colin. She gave her address, arranged the time and they talked for a wee bit. The conversation was open and warm, just as she liked it.

The following day Julia Sinclair went out to the shops and bought a kilo of Chicken fillet, cream and some rice. She had the rest of the stuff in the house. She wasn't sure if Gary was a drinker but since he lived in Glasgow she thought the odds against him not were about 100:1, so she bought six beers- a mixture of real ales. She felt lovely. Standing up to Colin at last and some cash coming her way soon she was sure. She was in no doubt Colin would pay to protect his cherished reputation. As she finished her shopping, Julia Sinclair failed to see Ringo, follow her as she headed homewards. Ringo had trailed her from the moment she had left the house. It was going to be done there, so he wanted to see the house and surrounds. It was his first time to kill, but he felt oddly detached and relaxed. The target was old, but she had a spring in her step and was still attractive. Colin had not explained why he had to do this job, but Ringo guessed that had had an affair, which had become complicated and he wanted her silenced. Fair enough. Not his problem. He followed Julia home from a distance and then walked past her house. Ringo turned at the junction at the end of her street and stopped. He soon saw it. A couple of hundred yards down the road he saw a pub and a guy standing outside clutching a cigarette. 'Ok, there's my alibi, if needed,' he thought, nodding in satisfaction. No supermarket too close either. If ever traced to the area he calculated he could say he was in the pub the whole time and would make sure people would be able to recall the fact. 'The Master planner,' he smiled to himself.

CHAPTER 8

Her train arrived in Glasgow late and Liz got a taxi to the Hilton. She was back where she belonged and she was going to figure this bastard thing out. She felt safe enough for the moment booked into the Hilton. She had asked the Receptionist staff to make sure that if anyone did happen to enquire if she was staying to deny it. She got to her room, dumped the rucksack on the bed and ran a bath. Despite all, she was glad she had made the decision to come home and a hotel was reassuringly safe compared to an isolated caravan in the Highlands. She wallowed in the bath and her thoughts drifted. She longed to go out and walk around her City just to be around people again, but...

She had taken the risk and left the hotel for a bit of shopping and a coffee. She was walking in Sauchiehall street. The rain came down. The sky was blue grey. Hundreds of people were walking around the street. Glancing upward she saw William Ware standing motionless looking at her. Liz stopped, looked around and ran. Willie stared to run towards her. She ran down West Campbell street. She looked back. No sign of him. She saw an alleyway with a large bin, ran to it and crouched behind it. She could hear own heavy breathing above the sounds of the bustling city and the rain. Through the space between the bin and the wall she peered anxiously for any sign of Ware. She saw him run by the alley. Liz thought of Stuart and her home as tears welled up. She was too scared to move yet. Then behind her she heard one word, 'Hoare' as a large, powerful hand grabbed her on the shoulder and spun her round. Willie was standing there. His eyes were cold and he held a knife in his hand which he raised to strike. Liz tried to move, but felt the knife pushing through her skin below her shoulder. She saw a spurt of blood as Willie raised the knife again. It felt warm. 'Hoare', he repeated. She saw Ian Smith on the ground behind Ware, His legs were crumpled and jutting out in weird angels, but he was dragging himself towards her. 'You are in danger,' he called out. 'Willie has lost it...'

Liz grabbed the handle of the large green bin and shoved it towards Willie. Unbalanced the knife came down ripping through her sleeve, gashing her arm. Ian reached Ware and grabbed his ankle. Willie turned to him. 'Hello Ian, back so soon?' then thrust his knife into Ian's back and turned again to Liz. She knew this time she was finished. He raised the knife and then Liz saw Stuart and Anne running towards them and then an explosion of colours and sound...

Liz sat upright in the bath, water splashing onto the floor with the force of her action. Her head darted around the bathroom and she felt her heart pounding as she sat there as the reality of the dream dissipated. She felt the warmth of the water, the blood...'Jesus,' she muttered and got out of the bath. She dried herself and ordered a large whisky from room service, deciding that her plan to walk around the town was not such a great idea after all.

Morris, Kevin and Stuart Hislop were back in Glasgow and having a drink in the Doublet.. On the way down Hislop had been subdued, Kevin – sprightly – in anticipation of his sister returning in a few days and meeting a pal that night and Morris felt things had gone great with Linda and was equally relaxed. As they sipped their drinks and chatted, Morris' thoughts drifted back to William Ware in Lochinver. Was he still there? He was skeptical of the story he had told him about his reason for the trip. And then there was what he had seen in the pub. The coincidence of meeting Ware had been too great. Kevin finished his drink and headed back to the flat. Morris turned to Stuart.

'I was just thinking about Willie,' he said.' I know he's your best pal and all that but could I ask you something?'

Hislop nodded. 'Sure, go ahead.'

'Well, just before I went to Linda's place I looked in the pub again. He looked pretty smashed and talking to some teenage boys. They looked uncomfortable and then he placed his hand on one of the guy's knees. Look it's probably nothing, or even important, but do you think he is gay? He never married did he?'

Stuart laughed. 'Funny you should say that. I have always wondered the same. Liz reckoned he was. Anne too, she told me. Actually, Willie says he hates gays, but some of the things he said and the way he looked at me sometimes were a bit weird. Not that it bothered me. Each to his own.'

'Looked at you?' Morris said surprised.

'Yep. In particular, one night we were drunk and I hardly remember it, but he definitely came a bit too close and said something silly like I would always be in his heart. I think he even said something like he would wait for me. Something weird anyway. Usual best buddies type drunken declaration, but it was the nearness and tone and how he looked at me that was a bit different. All forgotten about the next day of course and it didn't change our relationship. The girlfriends he had…he was always strained with them especially when we were all out together. He would put them down. 'Bitches-all the same,' he often called them in private. Aye, a bit of a mixed up guy, but nevertheless he helped me and is a good pal. It doesn't affect anything does it anyway?' Hislop looked at Morris closely.

'No, not at all. Just the more I know, the more I might be able to figure out what's going on. Ian too. He and Ware were never close in that sense?'

'No, as I said, outwardly Willie was pretty antagonistic. 'Bloody poofs,' he often said. I'm not sure he ever actually went with a man, if he was gay. Ian was more reticent. Outgoing and a bit flamboyant, but he seemed as interested in women as the next man. You say Anne told you he had an affair with another man called Frank? Well, I don't know who that would have been. Anyways, it might just be Anne trying to reconcile herself with his leaving her. She's pretty messed up these days with the drink, so she could have made it up. I'd say there was a good chance of that.'

'No. I think it was genuine. I could see the hurt. I think another wee chat with Anne would be a good idea though,' Morris said.

Stuart stared out the Doublet's window for a minute. 'I just wish Liz would come back…' Hislop muttered and the conversation petered off.

CHAPTER 9

Ronald 'Ringo' Dunn had parked his car a few streets from where Julia Sinclair lived. He got out walked to the junction which turned onto the street leading to her home. Looking around for a place to observe that was concealed he saw an oak tree that looked suitable and moved behind it. He reached for his cigarettes and lit up, keeping an eye on the roads to and from Julia's house. He didn't like it much. The street was too open. Too many cars and people moving on and around the street. There was a chance someone could see him. A good chance. He chastised himself for his presumption that an old lady would be living in a quiet, secluded area. Now how could he get into Julia's place without being seen? He decided to wait till it was later, when the passing cars from people returning from work would be less. He lit up another cigarette and waited. Dunn noticed a man approaching Julia's door holding flowers and a bottle of wine, chapping the door and talking to Julia when it was answered. It was 17:30.

Subconsciously Dunn noted that the visitor was about the same height and build as him. Not too much difference in age. Suddenly an idea jumped into his thoughts. The way to get into her house, without suspicion being laid on him. In his own mind it was a brilliant plan and he envisaged proudly telling Colin after the job was done. He looked closely at what Scott was wearing, nodded and turned quickly, walked to Maryhill road and soon enough saw what he was looking for. A charity shop. He bought a light blue suit jacket and a pair of grey trousers. The dark blue umbrella he found in the third shop he went into. He stuffed the items into a black hold all he bought and headed back to his vantage point. He had been away half an hour and was confidant the visitor would still be in the house. It was now 18:02. Dunn prepared himself for the wait, lighting up cigarettes almost one after another. This was the part he could not predict, but he needed to see the old guy leave the house. It was nearly two hours later when he did so. Ringo moved quickly from his discrete vantage point. He headed in the direction of the pub he had identified earlier 'The Wee Slope' and soon found a place near it where he could hide his black bag. He did so and then headed to the pub. He walked in. A young guy in dungarees was at the bar sipping beer and chatting to the barman.

Perfect. Dunn sat a couple of stalls for him and he and the barman and drinker engaged in banal conversation. It was 20:15. He had been there fifteen minutes.

'I'm going for a smoke,' he announced standing up and patting his right side trouser pocket. 'Shite, I must have left my fags at the last pub. Bugger. You guys know any shops or supermarkets where I can get some. He opened his wallet. I'll need to get to an ATM as well…price of fags these days.'

The barman spoke.

'Aye, a wee bit away though. Go out the pub and turn right and then first left. There is a co-op about half a mile away up Maryhill road. Fags are a bit cheaper in there. ATM there as well…'

'Thanks a lot.' Ringo replied, heading for the door. After walking out the pub casually, he moved swiftly to the hiding place took the bag and went into an empty alley way to change. When he turned the junction leading to Julia's house he opened the umbrella and covered his head with it.

It was quiet – no one in the street at the moment. 'Good,' he thought. 'It's afterwards I need someone'.

Ringo Dunn chapped on the door. It was 20:25. He heard the movement towards the door and then.

'Who it is there?'

'Hi. This is John O'Neil. I have a delivery for a Ms. Julia Sinclair. From an admirer I was told to tell you.'

'A delivery for me? Who from? she asked, but she was smiling. She had had such a nice time with Gary and it looked like he had sent her something. 'How lovely…'

'Hold on,' she said and undid the latch, opening the door. As she did so, she looked momentarily surprised as the man in front of her was dressed exactly the same as Gary had been and even had the same umbrella.

The man in front of her smiled, but was holding no gift in his hand. He was wearing gloves though…

He let down the umbrella and moved one step towards her and frightened she stepped back. But it was too late. Dunn shoved her back so strongly that she fell back. In a second he was on top of her and had his hands round her neck. He kicked the door shut from the floor. Julia gasped and then tried to struggle, but within seconds she felt the life being drawn out of her. She had quick flashes of her son on his wedding day and her daughter walking through the woods with Julia behind full of love…

When he was sure she was dead. Dunn moved quickly to the kitchen first and seeing nothing there that he wanted, moved to the lounge. There on the table was two empty wine glasses. One was placed in front of a chair to the side of which on another table was a pair of glasses, a book and a newspaper. He dragged Julia into the room and placed her on the couch where he calculated she had sat earlier. He placed her left hand over the arm of the couch and gently pushed over the wine glass and disturbed the newspaper and book, the latter falling to the floor. Then he picked up the other glass with his gloved hands, broke it at the side of the table where the old guy would have sat and shoved it into her throat. He watched the blood escaping from her dead body. He felt nothing. He took off his gloves. He reached down and wiped some blood onto his hands and grey trousers where he hoped it would be noticed. He moved away and looked around the room.

'All done and good,' he thought feeling a lot calmer than he thought he would be. It was 20:45, he noticed, glancing at his watch. The next part of his plan relied on a bit of luck, but if he pulled it off he felt he would be in the clear he believed. He went to the side of the front window and looked up to the top of the street. It was quieter now, but after five minutes he saw a car turning into Julia's street. He moved quickly to the front door, opening it and the umbrella at the same time. He covered his face with it again. It was drizzling. Good. He saw the car was about fifty meters away. With his face still almost completely covered by the umbrella he then walked straight onto the road. The car was no more than fifteen meters away now and screeched to a halt. Ringo raised his hands in apology. The blood on them could be clearly seen. He walked quickly back to the alley way, removed his killing clothes and wiped off the blood that had seeped on his hands. He paused to catch his breathe. He would pick up the bag after the pub and dispose of it safely after.

Five minutes later he was back in the pub. It was a couple of minutes before nine. He had been away three quarters an hour.

The barman glanced up. The young drinker had left.

'All sorted? Price of fags these days…'

'I know. Bit of a walk and queue at the ATM, but all good. Thanks for your help pal. Fancy a pint? Nine o'clock nearly already. Only three hours till closing…'

It was the next day when Julia was discovered. Every couple of days she had popped round to her friend three houses down the road for a tea and a chat at lunchtime. When she did not come, the friend went round to the house and rang the bell and knocked on the door several times. Slightly concerned she returned home, but after several unanswered calls to Julia and another visit she called the police.

They were in no hurry to come, but when they did and also got no response they forced the door after assurances by the neighbour that something seriously must be wrong and entered and soon walked the lounge.

Frazer, in his office in Dumbarton road, was just leaving for the day when he was informed of the murder. It was in his jurisdiction, less than a mile away, so he organised a lift to the house. Forensics were already at work and three officers mingled and spoke to the neighbours. He took one look at the scene and surmised a murder, but was experienced enough to wait till it could be confirmed.

He asked forensics for a quick opinion.

'Argument looks like. Two people. The killer attacked her on the couch and shoved a wine glass into her throat. Also signs of compression to the neck. Killer tried to strangle her too…. Strange though, looks like it could have been before…'

'Before the glassing?' Frazer queried. 'You think she was dead before the glassing?'

'Can't say for sure yet. Tell you post post-mortem…'

Frazer had seen a lot, but this was a bad one. An old lady for fucks sake. Glassed in the throat. Thankfully it looked like a spur of the moment killing and prints would still be on the wine glasses- more easy to catch the killer. 'Who are you, you cunt?' Frazer said to himself grimly. 'I'm coming for you, you bastard…'

The killing was front page news on all the papers the next morning. Ringo and Colin Shaw were up first thing at their separate homes to gauge the police reaction and any suspicions. Looked good they both surmised. Shaw later deposited the second payment in Ringo's account as arranged. Lorna Boyd at Far Away travel agency on Byres road only became aware of the death during her lunch break.

'Oh my God, poor Julia,' she gasped on reading the report. The reports did not state how she had died, but were clear that it was a murder case. The police were, as usual, appealing for anyone who may have any information. Suddenly it dawned on Boyd that only a couple of days ago she had giggled over the phone with Julia and said how nice and good looking Gary Scott was and that she should contact him, offering his number that she had taken from him. She had phoned back the next day to tell Lorna that he was coming for dinner and how she was so excited by it.'

'The same time she was killed. No, not him, surely…?' she now thought.

Initially she dismissed the possibility, but on getting back to the agency decided it was best to call the police.

An hour later Frazer was informed that Gary Scott, pensioner had had a dinner date with Julia the same night she had been murdered. He slapped the table. They had his phone number and had already traced it to Park Road at Kelvinbridge.

'Bingo. Good stuff. Speak to this Boyd woman. Get the bastard and bring him in. This is looking good for a quick solve…thank God.' He thought briefly of the consequences for him too. The Hit and Run case had got nowhere and upstairs were none too pleased, so this would help balance his reputational book. Not that he had done anything wrong Investigation wise, but that's the way it works. Quick solve, he was in charge, everyone praising the police, everyone pleased and happy…splendido.

An hour later Gary Scott had just got back from Lidl's when the doorbell went. He hadn't seen a newspaper or seen the news yet and was taken back to see two burly officers standing in front of him. 'Gary Scott…'

Frazer decided he would do the interview. If he admitted it, it was one of the aspects of the job he most liked, prizing guilt out of smug bastards. He entered the interview room with relish. Before him sat an old, disheveled and confused looking old man. Frazer was not swayed. He knew it took all types. Just before going in to the room, a quick background check had been handed to Frazer which showed that Scott had been in the army in Northern island and the Falklands. Two years after his leaving he had been charged with assault. The victim, his girlfriend. 'Temper, temper,' thought Frazer, ordering details of the incident to be sent to him as soon as possible. He strode into the room and met Scott's eyes dead on. Looking at his demeanor and confusion, Frazer decided on the softer approach, at least to start with.

Completing the interview formalities and sitting directly opposite Scott while an officer stood at the door he leaned slightly closer and effected a sympathetic tone.

'… so you live in Park road. How long have you been there Scott?'

'Eh, twelve years I think. Yes, 2009 it was, when I moved in that is.'

'You live alone?'

'Yes, just the dog…'

'Ah. Nice. Scott, we have some questions about where you were two days ago and we need some details of what you did. OK?' Frazer was eyeing him closely. The day of the murder, but not a flicker.

'Well, I went to a lady's house for dinner. But nothing really happened.'

'Rather odd comment' thought Frazer, continuing. 'And the ladies name was Julia Sinclair?' He thought this might get Scott to wondering how the police knew where he had been. Put the pressure on a wee bit.

'Well, yes, that was her name. How did you know that? You been following me?' he laughed.

Rather than stretch it out, Frazer thought it was time to push things along.

'And you had dinner as you said and then what? You left? And she was fine when you left.'

'Aye, I was there for about two hours and then walked up the road and then later into The Doublet for a quick one as I was feeling happy. I don't normally go so late…' Scott straightened up and looked around the room.

'Has something happened to her? Is she ok? This is all a bit strange.'

'She is dead Gary,' Frazer said, almost matter of factly, letting it hang in the air. Scott's eyes widened and he let out a small gasp.

'Oh Jesus. Oh no. that's awful. When did this happen?' He did look surprised Frazer noticed, but possibly he had been preparing to be so.

'Funnily enough, about the same time that you were there the forensics guys are saying. So Gary, just tell us what happened exactly there. You had dinner, a glass of wine…?'

'Jesus ta fuck. This is awful. Excuse my language, but it's a shock. She was fine, what happened- a heart attack or something?'

'Gary, she was murdered…you didn't see it in the news, or papers?'

'Murdered….and you think me? It wisnae. I don't watch TV, or read the papers much. This is awful…'

There was an urgent knock on the door. The officer opened it, listened to the information being passed and moved quickly to Frazer whispering in his ear. Frazer stood up.

'Excuse me Gary, hold on a sec. Just tell us what happened when I get back. Better to get it all cleared up now.'

He went at the door and read the paper he had been handed.

'Gary Scott. 02.12.1946. Charged with Grievous Bodily Harm 16.03.2006. Victim Mary Wells. They had lived together for five years. Broken nose, collar bone and arm.' Frazer's eyes opened wide and he nodded as he read the next lines. *'Twenty-five stitches caused by a slash across the cheek. Location- Mary Wells house. Newcastle Upon Tyne. Verdict. Guilty. Sentenced to three years. Released 18.07.2009. No other misdemeanors found.'*

'As usual, looks can be deceiving' he thought. 'He was experienced enough to know that what he had been given was no proof per se, but it did show what this seemingly quiet, congenial, man was capable off.'

He was just about to head back into the interview room, when he got a call. He was not going to take it, but saw the caller was Dr. Howard Johnstone- the forensics guy.'

'Hi Howard. I'm interviewing the suspect right now. Have you got anything- be quick.'

'Yes, I'm fine thank you', came the sarcastic reply. 'Ok. We were as quick as we could be. We got the prints from the Wells case. They match with one of the wine glasses. The one with blood on it....'

Frazer clenched his fist,

'...Second bit is a bit difficult. Definite compression to the neck region and she may have been killed first and then glassed, but not 100 per cent on that one yet. Both happened about the same time though, I can tell you that much. You are dealing with one sick bastard.'

'They all are Howard. They kill in many ways, but it's always malicious and cruel. Ok, that's great work and thanks'. He put the phone back in his pocket and reentered the interview room. Scott was just staring at the wall, his hands clasped together at the knee.'

'Ok Gary. I have just received some more information and it's not looking good for you I'm afraid. Heat of the moment thing was it…? Just get it off your chest. It will be better. Tell us the whole thing now please.'

Scott stuttered and raised his hands as if pleading for mercy already.

'Ok, ok. This is crazy. I met her again. I used to know her and remembered where she worked. Byres road- in a travel agency. I summoned up the courage and went there. She didn't work there anymore, but the manager, Lorna Boyd, said she would contact her and see if she would see me again. You see, I used to go there to book my holidays and we got along well. I was really surprised, but Julia agreed to see me and asked me to go for dinner. I was a bit shell shocked- had not even been near a lady for a meal, or drinks for years after…'

'After what Gary?'

Frazer was a little surprised that Scott seemed to be opening up so readily.

'I was involved in a bad one, in Newcastle, before. I went to prison for three years because of it. I sort of vowed to remain single after I got released, but then I saw Julia and I just wanted to meet her again. It's hard to say...'

'You are talking about Mary Wells before...?

'Yes, that was her name,' Scott said, looking surprised. 'I was wrong to do what I did and paid a price for it, but she was the most eveil women I had ever met. She had already abandoned her first two kids and when I saw what she had done to her five-year-old son- the wee boys face was battered black and blue- a few drinks and the army training came out. Anyway, I paid the price, I served my time. But if you think I would have harmed Julia, you have got the wrong end of the stick. We just chatted, had a meal, a glass of wine- well I had a couple of beers too- and then I left around eight.'

Frazer had done the nodding in empathy routine as Scott spoke. Now he straightened up.

'Ok, Gary. Just tell us a wee bit more about Julia. Can you tell us what you did before and after going to her place and what times these happened? It might help'

Scott nodded enthusiastically, thinking in his mind he had almost already proved his innocence and imagining himself an hour or two later in the Doublet telling all that he had been interviewed at Dumbarton road police station. ('for murder, would you believe!').

'Aye, sure. Thank you. Well, I prepared myself in the flat. Had a bath and stuff. Went to the Doublet for some fortitude. Walked down Woodlands road to Charing Cross and found her place easily enough. I can remember dead on when I got there as she had said five thirty and I wanted to be spot on, so five thirty I got there. I had brought wine and she had bought some nice beers. Ales. We sat in the lounge and chatted away, it went well. She had made Chicken something or other and after that we went back to the lounge and chatted some more. I didn't touch her, or try to, I swear. We had another glass of wine and I thought it best to go before I bored her. I told her I had been in prison- but didn't give her the details…I thought that might be a bit much since I was alone with her in her house. Anyway, I was there for about two and a bit hours- left about eight, as I said. Walked back, went home for a while, took Rory for a quick walk and decided to have a night cap in the pub. I remember looking at the clock and it was about nine thirty and deciding to have one more. Bit late for me, but I was in a good mood. Ask in the pub. I'm sure I was there by nine at the latest.

'Ok, Gary. That's good. Just a bit weird that you suddenly decided to see Julia again after all these years. We will check what you said about the Travel agency and the pub, but just explain why you suddenly wanted to see her after what, ten years. It's a bit strange, as I'm sure you can see.'

'I moved to Newcastle in 2004 and never saw her when I came back, so it was a long time, but then I saw her again here by chance.'

'You bumped into her in the street again, or something. Where and when was this Gary?'

'Aye, just near my house. It was early in the morning round about five fifteen and I was taking Rory out for a walk. Rory is my dog, sorry. About a month ago I guess, maybe three weeks…she passed in her car, driving very fast. She looked terrified to be honest. I saw her, but couldn't place her, but I knew I knew her. She didn't recognise me I'm pretty sure.'

'We need a better date than that Gary. Try and remember…' Fazer insisted.

Scott thought for a moment. 'Ah,' he said. 'The next night in the pub I was talking to a guy called Phil Burns and he had said there had been an accident up at Kelvin Way and somebody was killed. Hit and run I think he said. He is a postman and had been in the area just before it happened apparently. Later that day that I remembered that just before I saw Julia in her car I had heard a noise like brakes and a thump around the top of Gibson street. I had forgotten about it already and shrugged it off when Burns told me. Does that help pin it down a bit. If you have the hit and run accident date that's the same date when I saw her.'

Frazer sat upright. He could not believe what he was hearing. Scott had seen Sinclair at five twenty about in the morning. He had heard loud car noises from the area where it happened. The body had been discovered just after …

'Gary. Did you not think of going to the police with what you heard and saw for Christ's sake?' Frazer said, thinking how much work time could have been spared if Gary had done so.

'I don't know. As I said I didn't know who the driver was at the time. I didn't see any hit and run, just heard a noise. I forgot about it to be honest and I don't read the news much as I told you.'

Frazer's mind was racing all over the place, but he had something at last. The only thing he could not fathom was why, if it had been an accident as it sounded like, Sinclair had not gone to the police.

'Gary, did you talk about this when you met for dinner?'

'We did. I mentioned it almost straight away but not about hearing any noises, just that I had seen her coming down Gibson street. She said it could not be her as she did not have a Mercedes. She had already told me she had had one before, but sold it. A blue one. That was the car I saw that day, did I say?'

'No you didn't' said Frazer, a little exasperated, but glad to hear he now had the car make as well and the same colour as the blue paint that had been found on Ian Smiths trousers.

'Anyway, I knew it was her,' Scott continued, 'but just let it go. She looked a bit nervous to talk about it, so I just left it...She was jittery too. I just said it was probably someone who looked like her, but was glad that it had made me remember her. I remember after that she smiled at that and then got up quickly to make the dinner. I could tell she did not want to discuss it anymore.'

There was another knock on the door. Frazer was again called out. He felt almost surprised at the news. Despite himself, he was being swayed by Scott's apparent honesty and had started to doubt his presumption of guilt.

The officer explained to him that a neighbor had been driving home and had nearly hit a man crossing the road. When the police asked him about it and described the clothes Scott had been wearing- described by witnesses at the Doublet- he confirmed that the man he almost ran down was wearing the same clothes and had the same blue umbrella. There had also been blood on his hands.

'That's it then' Frazer announced to the corridor. The officer who had informed him smiled. 'I wish they were all so easy guv. Well done.'

Frazer turned walked back into the room and charged a stunned Gary Scott with the murder of Julia Sinclair

Morris was stunned to read in the papers that Gary Scott had been charged with the murder. 'Can't be. No chance.' He had planned to give Frazer a call in the next day or two, but hastened the call. He liked Scott and was keen to see how he could possibly have been accused of murder. 'Julia Sinclair. Who the hell is she anyway?' he wondered.

'… it's pretty conclusive' Frazer told him when Morris eventually got through to him. 'He admits to being there, his prints were on the murder weapon and he was seen crossing the road with blood on his hands when he left the house. The description of what he was wearing matched. We asked at the Doublet and got conformation. He was also carrying a distinctive umbrella. You probably know him from the pub?'

'Yes, very well. It's hard to fathom. He is a lovely guy. Quiet. A bit sad and lonely, but I would never have put him down for a murder. Mind you he had been in prison for assault before. You know about that?'

'Aye, a pretty vicious attack, including a slashing. Its him alright, I reckon.'

'Who was the victim anyway?' Morris asked.

'Well, you will find this interesting. Julia Sinclair.'

'Don't know her, why interesting,' Morris asked puzzled.

'The hit and run when Ian Smith was killed…'

'You're kidding?' Morris said. 'Go on…'

'Well it looks like she was the driver. Scott had seen her in the car that day, that's what made him think of her again and tracked her down for a date. Anyway, he saw her in a car just after hearing a noise up at the Union. About five thirty he said which was the right time. Especially him saying he had heard a noise as well just before seeing her. He said she was driving fast and looking terrified. It must have been her. Why a seventy-year-old women should be driving around at five thirty in the morning I'm not really sure yet.'

'I have thought the same about Ian,' Morris said. 'What was he doing at that time there as well? You know that Ian was close to Stuart and Liz and it seems odd that she left more or less at the same time. The more I think about it I have a nagging feeling that the two things are connected.'

'Hard to see how. Liz was asleep according to Stuart Hislop- but it's a possibility.' Frazer said. 'Look got to go. Pint sometime soon?'

'Sure, sure. Still no word from Julia by the way. After the Lochinver stay, she just vanished again. We just missed her by a day. It was if someone told her that we were coming.' Morris said.

'Well. At least she is alright. Maybe just leave it a while? Sam, do you think you could talk to Anne again? You know her and she might open up a bit to you. Not that we have a lead again I want to get this solved. We have the suspect now although she is dead.

Now we want to see if it was an accident or not. Run Julia's name by Anne and see if there is reaction. Just in case. If you are suspicious enough we will bring her in for another chat. I can't help thinking she knows more than she is telling us. She was half cut the first time we talked to her. She might open up to you more than us.' Morris nodded into the phone. 'I'll arrange a meeting as soon as I can,' he replied.

CHAPTER 10

Anne Smith had just come out of the shower. After breakfast she had found herself drinking a couple of glasses of wine and in a moment of rare realisation chastised herself and poured the third glass down the sink. Surprising herself, she then poured the rest of the bottle down the sink as well. 'You are killing yourself for Christ's sake, so just bloody do it,' she had said, staring into the bathroom mirror and analysing her life. Emboldened she had stripped off and had a long shower, deciding to stop the boozing for as long as she could, whether it be a day, or a month. No targets, just a raw determination to do something. After a coffee she felt almost sober, but she noticed her hand was shaking a bit. She turned on the TV to pass the time and had made another coffee. Presently the news came on. The murder of Julia Sinclair was still prominent news. The police were now releasing further news the Chief Constable being interviewed declared. The victim, Julia Sinclair, in what was called 'an ironic twist' was the chief suspect for the Hit and Run incident in University avenue on 16th June. This is a result of information passed to the police. ….'

Anne sat up in amassment. 'Her?' she mused. 'An old woman. Five thirty in the morning. Didn't go to the police…? Ian killed by an old lady?' She shook her head. She had presumed it would have been a drunken teenager driving home after a party. She thought instinctively to have a drink, but pushed the thought out of her head. She was still watching keenly when her phone went. She saw the incoming call was from Sam Morris. She squirmed, remembering their last meeting. Nevertheless, she answered.

'Hi Anne. It's me again. How are you doing?'

'Oh, hello Sam. Nice of you to call. Doubted you would after my last performance. I'm sorry about that. I don't remember much after we left the Chip. I was sick for two days after. I'm really sorry.'

'If you don't mind me saying, maybe you should lay off the booze for a bit. You know you nearly swallowed your own sick. A great servant, bad master as they say…' Morris said.

'Have been thinking the same Sam. I just poured a bottle of wine down the sink in fact. I'll give it a go. Any news on Liz?'

Still keeping things close to his chest Morris replied in the negative. 'I'll let you know if we hear anything.' He said lamely. 'Anyway did you see the news about the Hit and Run and Ian. At least it looks like they have found the person that killed Ian. Bit of a surprise though. An old lady.'

'Just what I was thinking too, saw it in the news just now-was out of it yesterday,' said Anne. 'What the hell was she doing up and about at that time and presumably driving crazily. It's terrible that she is dead and can't tell anyone now.'

'You know the guy arrested for her murder goes to the Doublet a lot. Gary Scott. He is seventy odds for Christs sake, looks like he stuck a glass into her throat.'

'Jesus, that's bad. Do you know him from the pub?' Anne asked.

'Yes, pretty well. He is in, or was in, every day. Quiet guy. It's hard to believe, but the police say it's a hundred percent. Anyway, do you fancy a coffee later today, or tonight? Maybe a meal? Hopefully we will eat this time.' He laughed in a slightly sarcastic manner.

Anne Smith blushed and looked at her hand. It was trembling more than earlier. It was going to take some time, but she was going to do it. 'That would be lovely Sam. I haven't been out since my performance at our last meeting.' They arranged to meet that evening and try again at the Chip. Sam ended the call and booked a table for eight thirty. He then phoned Anne back and they agreed to meet outside the Chip and go straight for dinner. Morris spent the day pottering about and went for a walk with Kevin and a pal of his from work, before getting ready and having a couple of pints in the Doublet. He arrived outside the Chip at eight twenty-five. Anne arrived ten minutes later. She looked good and also sober. They went in and sat down at their reserved table. Anne was on the Diet cokes much to Morris' pleasant surprise. When Morris mentioned that he and Linda had got back together Anne smiled, but there was a slight sadness in her tone as she did so.

'I'm happy for you,' as the words trailed off.

'Thanks Anne. Can you tell us a bit more about Ian and this Frank guy- when did you get suspicious?'

'I saw a note Ian had left in his trouser pocket- yes I did search through his stuff I was already suspicious- he had been acting strangely for a couple of weeks. But I never thought he was having an affair with a man, so it was a real shock when I found it. It said 'Frank. Tennents. One thirty Thursday'. There was a love kiss at the bottom, which shocked me totally. I admit I went there. Ian stood outside the pub and a car pulled up and he got in. The windows were dark, so I could not see the driver…'

'They just drove away. When he got home that night I showed him the note. He tried to laugh it off, said it was just a mate from school and they used to joke around like that pretending that they were partners. He said he only loved me. I wasn't convinced of course, but somehow gave him the benefit of the doubt and let him stay. Desperation for it not to be true, I guess. But after I while I couldn't fool myself any longer. Every time I saw Ian there was guilt all over his face too. Eventually I threw him out. Don't know why he was walking around the streets at five in the morning though. Bit weird. Probably on a bender. Anyway, in the meantime, I had shagged a guy too, so it was over as far as I was concerned.'

Morris was taken aback. 'Oh. I see. You had a lover also.'

'No! I was hurting and full of hate. I wanted revenge. First day of May. I remember it. Soon after finding the note from this Frank guy, I went to the Doublet got drunk and let myself get picked up. An English guy would you believe. He was only up for a few days, so that suited me fine. Roy Shorrocks.' Morris raised his eyebrows in surprise at the fact he knew the guy and remembered Shorrocks saying something about meeting a woman in the Doublet, but he let Anne continue without making a comment. 'Ian was at home and we didn't want to spend fifty quid in a hotel, his daughter was with Roy and was at his Airbnb, so we went to Liz's place, although I never told him whose flat it was. It was just next door and I couldn't resist. I had spare keys to clean and water the plants when they are away in the Highlands. She was out working and she had told me that Stuart would be out drinking with an old friend and not back till late. I knew we would not need to be there long. It was a bit sordid, but we went to the flat, it was empty as expected and I slept with the guy. It was all over in ten minutes. After we went back to the pub. Stuart was there funnily enough. I remember thinking that it was a close shave that he hadn't come to the flat. He was drinking like a madman. Never seen him like that before…Anyway at home things got worse with Ian. His infidelity - my infidelity. I eventually threw Ian out. Next day after he is dead and I still feel the guilt…'

As the story unfolded Morris realised the implications with astonishment. The beginning of May! It had not been his wife that Stuart had heard in the bedroom when he opened the front door. It had been bloody Anne! That was the time when he heard who he thought was Liz. Stuart's whole bases for distrusting his wife and his subsequent behaviour towards her had been based on a false premise. This changed everything, or it would for Stuart…

'Did you ever tell Liz about using her bed?' Morris asked excitedly, although he could guess the answer.

'What do you think? After I felt awful about it. No way I told her.'

'Well, I'll tell you now. Stuart came home and when he opened the door he heard what he thought was Liz in bed with another guy, but it was you. He just closed the door and went to The Doublet. So, when you saw him in there, he had just come from the house. After that, that's when the problems started between the two. He told me about it. So it was you after all. I'll need to tell him that all he thought about Liz was wrong.'

'Oh no, it was all due to me,' Anne cried out 'What have I done? They will never forgive me…'

'It was a pretty shit thing to do Anne. That can't be escaped, nor denied. But, it should help Stuart and Liz get back together and maybe after some time you will be forgiven.'

Anne slumped in her chair and sobbed. Morris remained quiet for a few minutes, then asked.

'Ok. You and Ian. You never found anything more about this Frank guy?' he asked.

Anne had drifted away, thinking only of what her actions had done to Liz and Stuart, but reengaged on hearing Morris's words.

'No…no, just that note and seeing Ian get in his car. He's probably still out there ruining someone else's marriage right now. Just like I bloody did…but I tell you if I saw him in the street there would be another Hit and Run to deal with. Bastard.'

'This Julia Sinclair that was murdered- looks certain that it was her that ran over and killed Ian. Know her-ever heard of her at all?' Morris said, watching Anne's reaction carefully.

Anne Smith shrugged and shook her head. 'No, never heard of her before the murder,' she said wiping some tears from her cheek.

They finished their dinner and since Anne was sober he walked her home. She said little. It was a lovely night with golden rays reflecting of the tenement's sandstones and spreading onto the roads and surrounds.

Morris dropped Anne off and decided to enjoy a walk back and do some thinking at the same time. There was a lot to take in. But he was getting closer to understanding it all. He could feel it in his bones. He phoned Stuart and they arranged to meet in the Doublet. Once they were there and after some small chat, Morris moved onto his meeting with Anne. '… so she told me that one night she went to the Doublet and met a guy. Roy Shorrocks would you believe- the Airbnb guy.'

'Oh that guy you met… aye ok,' Stuart replied, without interest.

'No, but the thing is Stuart, she went back to your place with him. She knew you were supposed to be out with a pal boozing and Liz was working at the restaurant, so she went to your place and did it there. It was the first of May.'

Stuart nodded and then stopped still. 'My place, May first… Jesus. Out with an old drinking pal- that was the day I came back early and heard Liz…'

'It wasn't her Stuart. It was Anne. Anne was shagging someone in your bed to save a few bob on a hotel. Pretty grim and more than a bit sordid, but it was not Liz you heard. Anne never mentioned it to Liz- I'm not surprised either. She said she saw you in here drinking like a fish when she went back here afterwards. That's the time for sure.'

'No...for fuck's sake Sam. It wasn't Liz. What have I done?'

'Don't let it get to you Stuart- I think it was a natural assumption, anyone would have concluded the same.'

'Wait a minute. Maybe Liz has got in contact with Anne and they have made up this story to get her off the hook.' Hislop said.

'No way. The way she told me, I could tell it was the truth. I'm good at seeing when someone is lying remember. It was my job. I believe her. Liz wasn't the one.'

'So, I have fucked up the whole thing. Oh, for fuck's sake. All the suspicions, the looks, the non-communication...' he slumped forward in his chair. 'She would never come back now anyway. Why didn't I just ask her...?'

'It's hard to just do that- to get your suspicions confirmed and then to hear the reasons behind the actions. No one wants to get hurt further. Look, if you play this right, explain to Liz and do all you can by way of apology, I'm sure you can get her back.'

Hislop nodded and smiled weakly. 'Still have to find her first. What is she going through? Shunned by her own husband. She has probably given up on me by now wherever she is. What a fucking idiot. If we find her, I'll try, and just hope I can explain properly...'

Straight after getting home, Morris gave Frazer a call, mentioned that it looked like Anne Smith had no prior knowledge of Julia Sinclair, nor knew anything more about Ian's lover, Frank, and asked if there were any updates re Gary Scott. Despite Scott's past and the substantial evidence against him, Morris could not convince himself of Scott's guilt. Firstly, Frazer told Morris that they had drawn a blank on the phone Liz had used to call Quita. It was old and had probably been lost. He then moved on to the Sinclair case. 'Well it's a murder Investigation as you know and even though it looks like we have the killer I can't tell you everything- you know that. I have a few doubts myself to be honest, but nothing to back them up. Generally, I still think he did it. Latest is that another neighbour saw him at the door. Clothing and all that matched, so it was him alright. Bit strange though. It was just ten minutes or so until he was seen crossing the road with blood in his hands. He must have left and come back if his arrival and departure time that he said was true. From the flat search, we see all the dishes and stuff indicating that he was there for a couple of hours, not just a few minutes as the witness time implies.'

'You are right. That does not match with the apparent time line at all. Interesting. The neighbour was sure of the time?'

'Yes, she remembered her daughter called her at about the same time and she checked the phone. She also said something interesting. She mentioned that after Sinclair answered the door Scott seemed to stumble inside, or maybe even pushed his way in according the neighbour. She was sure he was wearing gloves too.'

'Interesting indeed,' replied Morris. 'Something doesn't fit here…'

'I'm going to talk again to Scott, see what he can remember. It's possible he went earlier as all the evidence indicates and came back and then that's when he killed her.' Frazer added.

'Aye, possible I suppose, but the idea he had a nice meal, left came back and killed her in ten minutes or so and left, seems odd. Will be interesting to see what he says. I can't do anything to help?' Morris enquired.

'Of course you can't Sam. This is a murder investigation need I remind you. However, you have a knack of joining the dots, so have a good think about it. Unofficially a wee walk around Sinclair's place might help you connect these dots. I never said that though.

By the way- it's time we had a couple of pints. Sunday, Doublet at six?

'I'll be there after I do some dot connecting…,' smiled Morris ending the call.

The next day Morris was in town with Kevin for a bit of shopping. They sat having a coffee, not saying much. Morris thoughts were drifting, as he tried to 'join the dots' for Frazer regarding Julia Sinclair's murder and her probable killing of Ian Smith. Why the hell had she not just informed the police? He thought yet again of Gary Scott and started shaking his head. Despite all the evidence against him Morris could not be convinced. He pondered the possibility that someone had found out about Julia running over Ian and getting the ultimate revenge by killing her. It had been a pretty gruesome murder. He believed the two deaths were too much of a coincidence. There had to be a connection between the Hit and Run and Julia's murder. He thought of Anne Smith again, but he tended to believe her story that she had heard about the murder after the event and could think of no way that Anne could have found out who the driver was. 'But keep it in mind,' he said to himself. His thoughts drifted further. 'I need to find this Frank guy. He was Ian's new boyfriend and never came to the police to clear his name. Could he be connected in some way with Julia. – asked her to run over Ian? He dismissed this possibility immediately as ludicrous and unsupported by any connections, or information. As Morris and Kevin got up to leave, he picked up on two girls talking.

'…so I bought this lovely new dress. Great fit, red colour. Got to the party and straight away saw Caroline was wearing exactly the same one. Can you believe it- exactly the same clothes?'

Morris took the words in and paused - something had been planted in his mind.

CHAPTER 11

Anne Smith had been sober all of two days and was starting to feel better, despite her worry about telling Morris about her visit with Shorrocks to Liz's flat. The shakes had lessened and she was thinking clearly. The drinking urges had dissipated considerably. She thought about Ian and his betrayal and was also partly regretting telling Morris about her and Shorrocks. Now Stuart would know and eventually Liz. She felt awful. Her best friends. A sudden thought came to her. Maybe Liz already knew about it and that's why she suddenly ended contact. She dismissed it. Liz would have been none too pleased, but would have said something for sure –asked for an explanation. Same thing if she had left with another guy. She would have called and explained, or at least informed - Anne was her best friend. She remembered now that she had told Liz about Ian. She had been as shocked as Anne had been, but offered her as much support as she could. Not long after Anne had used her bed she had called Liz and she had mentioned that she had seen the note from this Frank guy and saw Ian getting into his car at Tenents. Liz had said something too, she recalled.

'…not just Ian, we all have our problems…'

'What do you mean?' Anne had replied.

'Stuart has been acting strange too. He barely talks and looks at me almost with contempt- sort of sneering at me. I have done something to annoy him, but can't think what it could be. We didn't have a big fight or anything- it was sudden. One day great, the next day shunned. Whenever I try and approach him, I'm just pushed away.'

'Sounds like a midlife crisis to me.' Anne had said. 'Get his mind back to the important things in life. All good in bed?'

'It was fine, yes, and then again suddenly no. He moved into the spare room without explanation. That's when it all started. The looks, the despising…'

'Maybe try and spruce things up a bit. Dress to remind him what he is missing.' Anne had suggested.

'Maybe worth a go, aye. Poor us Anne. You and Ian, me and Stuart- what's happening? Maybe Willie had the right attitude all these years. No commitment. Never seemed to want it. He's been phoning Stuart quite a lot recently. Maybe Stuart has told him what the matter is. What the hell have I done to deserve this Anne? I'm fed up.'

Now Anne pondered what to do. Despite her hurt at Liz's lack of contact and freed from the emotional quagmire of drunkenness, she could only come to the conclusion that Liz was safe, but still in some kind of trouble. Did she think someone was trying to harm her? Anne decided. Liz was her best friend and if this was the case, she would do all she could to help her. She immediately thought of Ware and his nasty remarks. Perhaps he would know why Stuart had rejected Liz and explain why he himself had turned against her? She rose from her chair and went to get her phone. She was feeling responsible and determined. She owed her best friend- big time. When Anne, got through to William Ware she got straight to the point. 'Willie, that time we had a meal at the Shish, I want to ask you-why were you so nasty whenever Liz's name was mentioned. She and Stuart were all our good friends, but you were almost sneering in contempt whenever her name was mentioned. Liz noticed it as well, so I want to know now. She has gone and maybe your remarks had something to do with it. I'm pissed off.'

Ware thought quickly. He was trying to get to Liz to shut her up and here was Anne mentioning his hatred to Liz after Stuart had told him she had betrayed Stuart with another guy in Stuarts bed. He would be a suspect if something happened to Liz. It was clear in his mind. She had betrayed Stuart. Bitch deserved all that she would get. Now her friend Anne was poking around…

Before he could reply a forceful Anne continued. 'While we are getting things all sorted out here Willie, I want to ask you. Ian was gay. He was having an affair with a guy called Frank. Did you know about that, being a fellow gay…?'

Ware had a rush of blood to his head and his fist tightened into balls. Did she know? How did she know? Maybe Ian had texted her, not Liz after all. Somehow he had to get a grip of this conversation and quick.

'I'm sorry you feel that I am gay Anne. I was surprised to find out as much as anyone that Ian was, but not me, I'm afraid. Not a big fan to be honest and I often make that clear. Ian phoned me on the night he was killed. Staying in a hotel. He was drunk and confused. Ian was my friend and I hoped I could talk him out of it…'

'Talk him out of it?" What do you mean by that?' Anne replied angrily.

'Well, maybe it was just a phase and he would come back to you. I had your interest at heart. He was confused. He did mention this Frank guy. He had only seen him a few times though.'

'He was Ian's lover for fucks sake. I saw a note from him and saw them together.'

Ware could hear the pain in her voice. Maybe he could use that, if he did some lying.

'Look Ian told me that this Frank guy had been a mistake and he felt terrible what he had done to you. We talked and he said that he wanted to get back to you, but was terrified that you would reject him. I really think he meant it. About Liz- I'm really sorry for that. Stuart had told me she was acting strange and a bit hostile and you know Stuart and I go way back- so I was angry with her for making Stuart so upset. I know it was none of my business, but sorry, I couldn't help it. I just wanted all my best friends to be happy same as before…' He made his voice break and trail off. 'Not bad at all,' he thought to himself.

Anne listened in astonishment about Ian. In her anger and hurt she never contemplated that Ian could just be having an aberration – an experiment of sorts. Possibly he had still loved her. It still hurt, but maybe it could have been mended. Her eyes filled with tears.

'Oh Willie, I feel the same. Why did it all happen? I'm so down and upset. You said you talked to him on the night he was killed? I thought you would have mentioned that before? What else did he say… Look, can you come over tonight and we can talk more? I wish I had called you before now. It's all so confusing. Ian, Liz - not contacting me.'

Ware replied quickly. 'Stuart told me she hadn't even contacted you. I'm a bit worried for her. I even went up north to help find her, but no luck. She has never given you a call- not even once? Anyway, good idea. I'll come over right now. Let's keep it a secret till we figure what to do. I'll bring some of the wine you like too.'

'Thanks Willie, we can have a good talk. Bring two bottles…'

William Ware moved swiftly in thought and body as he tried to finalise his plan. Anne was getting way too close. Maybe Ian had texted her and not Liz and mentioned their sleeping together and that's why she had called him gay. Had she maybe told Stuart? Shit. He remembered the night with Ian again. Every moment was hardwired into his brain as he remembered. He was in his Glasgow flat in Hynland. Ian had phoned and talked about his situation from a hotel and Ware had told him to come to his place to have a drink. When he got to Ware's flat he started talking about it all straight away. He had not meant to hurt Anne and still loved her, but had just met Frank one day when he was at a casino and had found himself attracted to him. They had had sex the first night they had met and Ian said it had been wonderful. It just spiraled out of control after that. In the end Anne had found a note from Frank according to Ian, followed him and seen them together and then that night had said she had had enough and threw him out. Surprising himself, Ware had started thinking of Ian with another man-this Frank- and found he was getting excited. He had had this feeling before, but it had never gone further. This night though, something was different. Ian was vulnerable and tears welled in his eyes when he told Ware that Frank had not contacted him in a week and his phone was off. They had drawn closer to each other and then, after a moment's hesitation, kissed. Soon they were in bed.

After, the guilt started. Ware felt disgusted with himself, and started to take it out on Ian who was lying curled up at the other side of the bed.

'Ian, I don't know what happened there. I'm not gay, it was just a thing…'

Ian laughed, raising himself. 'That's what I thought too. Listen Willie, I was with you just now. Remember? Just accept it. At least you do not have a marriage to destroy and break someone's heart. You are lucky pal. Just get over it. He glanced at the clock. 'Fuck, its nearly five. I had better go.' he got up and dressed. 'I'll walk home- save the taxi money. University Avenue then Bank street quickest way from here to Kelvinbridge?'

Ware just nodded as Ian got ready to go. The bile was rising. Someone was walking out on him again. Like his mother had done. Leaving him with his bastard father. Then he made a mistake.

'So, you are just leaving then. Anyway, since it's all coming out now, let me tell you that I don't fancy you at all. It was just a primitive urge, so forget it and don't tell anyone, or I'll smash your fucking head in.'

Ian stopped and turned round in shock. Then he smiled. 'It's ok Willie, I know what you are going through. It was just a one-night thing. Let's not get over excited or dramatic about it all eh?'

Ware stood up to his full height. 'Yes, you run away. What a shame Frankie baby seems to have dropped you. Poor wee, sad Ian. Poof.'

'Fuck you too Willie,' said Ian, his anger increasing.

'Let me tell you Ian, I already love someone, one day we will be together and you even know him well. Surprise, surprise.'

'Him?' Ian said.

'Yes, him…Stuart.'

Smith had stared in astonishment but could not help himself letting out a laugh. 'Boy are you mixed up pal. Thought I was bad. You are in love with Stuart? Since when?'

'Since the first day I met him, 'Ware said proudly.

'But Willie, Stuart is not gay. You know that surely. He loves Liz, that's bloody obvious to anyone.'

'Aye and look how she is treating him. She fucked someone in his bed. Did you know that? Some wife. Fucking bitch. He deserves someone who will really love him,' Ware said his fury evident.

'I don't believe that for a second. You are making it up.' Ian said shaking his head.

'No I'm not. Stuart was there. He came home and heard her. Nice wife eh? Poor Stuart has been devastated ever since. It breaks my heart to see him like that. Anyway, I'm going to sort out his problem for him. You like Liz do you? Well she's not going to be around much longer. Permanent kaput. Now get the fuck out of my house and run away back to Frank- if he will have you.' Ware sneered.

'Oh, I'm going alright. By the way, you touch Liz in any way it will be you in the hospital, or worse. Up yours too pal.'

Ian had slammed the door and left, walking quickly. He was thinking rapidly. Ware had scared him, he admitted to himself. Would he do any of the things he had threatened? Ware had spent a life time decrying homosexuals. Now that had blown up in his face. He had seen the reaction. Self-loathing and hatred. He feared this could be channeled towards Liz. He was in love with Stuart. 'No chance there pal…'. However, in Ware's eyes, Liz could be seen as the unfaithful women deserving of removal for her act and clearing the way for Ware and Stuart to be together. 'Fucking nut case,' Ian concluded. He had stopped for a minute. Decided. He took out his phone and messaged Liz, warning her. He would meet her tomorrow and tell her everything. 'Maybe a bit dramatic, but best to be safe,' he concluded and continued om his way.

When he neared Kelvin Way, he heard the sound of running behind him. Glancing round he saw Ware jogging towards him. He shouted out a warning and mentioning he had seen Ian texting earlier. He looked like a crazed man. Instinctively, Ian started running himself, checking behind as he did so. He started to cross the road. He had heard a car and turned towards it...

Ware saw the car thud into Ian. He fell on his head and it was clear he was dead. He stopped in his tracks and looked. The driver was a woman. Old. There was complete silence for a moment. Then a dog parking somewhere. Ware could hear his own breath and his heart pumping. He immediately decided to get back to Stirling today, turned and started walking back up the hill. But the women in the car had probably seen him. He had seen Ian texting something near Tennents pub. What had he written and who was he sending it to? Maybe he was trying to contact this Frank guy, or worse Liz. That would ruin everything. He thought of running back and getting Ian's phone, but that would only give the driver a better view of him.

Ware had watched as the lady started to get out of the Mercedes. Then she stopped and looked around. It was clear she had seen him. His pace quickened. The driver turned back to her car, closed the door and drove around the body and turned into Gibson street driving fast. Ware contemplated again running back and getting the phone, but it was too risky. No, he had to get away. He packed and was back in Stirling by eight that morning.

Now, as he approached Anne Smith's flat he found his thinking was clear. Ian was dead. He would get rid of Anne tonight. She knew too much. In Lochinver one of the locals had told him that Liz had been staying in a caravan. He found it, but she had gone when he went there. Next time… If he found Liz and got rid of her there would only be Stuart and himself left. They could be together, platonically, or otherwise. It didn't matter- it was more than a sexual thing. It was love. He would let Stuart decide but Ware knew he would be happy just to be with him. He had liked Anne though, but that was before she had called him gay, just like his bastard father. He shrugged. 'So be it.' He rang the doorbell.

CHAPTER 12

Frazer was in the Doublet with Morris, updating him on the Sinclair murder. 'We talked to Gary again and he was adamant that he never returned to the flat and never had a near miss with a car crossing the road. We told him that the descriptions matched him exactly, but he just shook his head and said we and the witness had made a mistake. He actually looked quite relieved.'

'Your guys checked the Doublet and he was there at the time he said? Nobody in the pub said he was acting strange, or nervous- different?'

'No. he got in about nine. They all agreed he was in a great mood. He even mentioned to a few of them that he had been on a date with a wonderful lady. Mentioned her name too.'

'There you go. It doesn't fit well. A murderer would not just stroll into a pub and be able to act as if nothing had happened and talking casually about someone he had just killed. With all due respect, you can say what you want, but I know him and it all doesn't match. I don't think he killed Julia Sinclair.'

'I have my doubts too now after the last interview, but he was identified at the scene remember the exact same clothes with blood on them and his hands…so?'

Morris stopped for a second looking straight at the gantry.

'What's up?' said Frazer.

'Wait a minute -I was down town with Kevin yesterday having a coffee. I overhead a conversation where a girl was complaining that someone was dressed just like her. Maybe it wasn't Gary, just someone dressed the same. Could it be?'

'Naw,' said Frazer. 'He was dressed too distinctively. Even had a distinctive umbrella. Chances of another killer happening to be dressed the same would be millions to one.'

Morris sat upright and banged his fist on the table. 'Unless he knew what Gary was wearing and dressed the same, to place suspicion on Gary?!'

Frazer's eyes darted around the room. 'Fuck sake, could be, but how would he know though?' he said.

'The killer must either have known that Gary would be going to Julia's flat and knew what Gary would be wearing, or saw him going into the flat and went and bought the same clothes somewhere and went to her flat after Gary had left. There was time.' Morris said speaking rapidly now. 'Yes, yes, and then after he kills Julia, he deliberately walks in front of a car showing blood on his hands but covering most of his face with the umbrella to point the blame and Gary. Bastards. It all fits. Smart though, have to give him that.'

'Well, it's still a presumption, but it does sound plausible, I'll give you that. So, if that is how it was, the only conclusion we can surmise from this is that this was no argument. Someone deliberately wanted to get rid of Julia. But why? She was just an old lady for Christ's sake- no harm to anyone.' Said Frazer.

'It's got to be connected to the hit and run. Surely. Couple of questions about that. Why would she not report it to the police. She panicked obviously, but why?'

'Maybe pissed?' suggested Frazer.

'Aye, but would think it would take more than that for her to just abandon a body. No, I think she was scared of something else. The time thing as well. Five thirty in the morning, driving her car? Where the hell had she come from? We need to find that out. How you can do that I don't know. Maybe she was coming back from a trip somewhere. From the airport?'

'No, the neighbours saw her the night before leaving the house at around nine.' Frazer replied.

'Did any of them say they had seen her coming back early doors ever?'

'Not sure we asked that. We can check. That could help.'

'If you want I'll go and ask around. Unofficially of course…Just ask a few questions,' Morris suggested.

'Just keep a low profile. I didn't send you if anyone asks. You are a concerned friend of Gary's-ok?' Frazer said.

'No problem. Did Julia have an address book did you find?'

'She did. Loads of names in it though. Since we thought we had the killer we haven't done much with it though.'

'Ok,' Morris replied. 'I would go through it carefully. Five thirty in the morning- the only thing that springs to mind is that she was returning early from staying overnight and at that time it sounds like it could be a lover, since she wasn't coming back from a trip.'

'Well, no one came forward after her murder to mention that they were having a relationship with her…' Frazer added.

'Exactly,' Morris replied. 'An illicit affair- something went wrong - sounds like to me. Keeping the association unrevealed. Sounds about right. I think you will find the lover in the address book, might take you a while to narrow it down though. You need to locate and talk to him, or her.'

'Ok,' said Frazer. 'In my guts, I think you are on the right track. But convincing those upstairs of it – that's another matter. They won't be pleased – the case was solved- they will do their best not to be persuaded of Gary's innocence. That's the way it works.'

Morris smiled slightly. 'The truth will out! Good idea to check if that girl at the travel agency who contacted Julia on behalf of Gary knows anything else. Maybe when the date was arranged she told someone else about it?'

'No, there we are good. When she contacted the police she mentioned that she had only told Gary that Julia had agreed to contact him. She never had occasion to mention it to anyone else even at the agency.'

'Ok. That's a blank then. The address book, you should look at that.' Morris paused for a minute. 'And I have some information about Ian as well. Anne told you she had thrown him out that night. She did so because Ian was having an affair with a guy called Frank- that's all she knows. Just the first name and no address or anything. Maybe he was with Ian that night and lives around University Avenue and could give you some background on Ian and especially why he was out at that time. Looks certain Julia was the driver, so can't see him as asuspect…but might help.'

'Right,' said Frazer downing the rest of his pint. 'I'm off. That was an interesting chat and looks like we are going places. I'll speak to the top brass and get the team to go through the address book. You have a sniff around Julia's street and see what you can come up with. Noted what you say about Ian's boyfriend. Thanks. I'll be in touch soon…going to dig a bit deeper into all this.'

Frazer left. Morris stayed, nursed his pint while planning what to do.

CHAPTER 13

Anne Smith waited patiently and determinedly for William Ware's arrival. He had thought he was smart on the phone, but she could tell he was lying through his teeth. She needed to know the whole story, but admitted to herself she was a wee bit scared of his visit. But she needed to sort this out for her sake and for Liz. She had told Ware to bring wine, emphasising two bottles for effect but she had no intention of having more than a sip while she listened to Ware. She was also scared enough to take a kitchen knife from the drawer and hide it behind a cushion next to where she sat on the sofa. 'Just in case…' The doorbell went. She rose with an affected calm and answered the door.

'Hi Anne.' said Ware grinning wildly. 'Great to see you again.' He raised his hand showing a bag from the off sales. 'Here you go- the good stuff.'

'Come in, come in,' She hugged him tightly adding to the sense of vulnerability she wanted to create.

Anne ushered him into the lounge and opened the wine and poured two glasses. Ware immediately took a large gulp. She just raised her glass, let it touch her lips and returned it to the table.

'I'm glad we have met,' Ware said. 'Everything is so confused now. Ian is dead, Liz has disappeared, Stuart seems a bit evasive to me lately and even you Anne were a wee bit hostile on the phone. I'm sort of under pressure, I feel I'm losing it a bit. If we could just say in life what we really feel wouldn't the world be a better place.'

'Anne nodded. 'I know what you mean. I also wish everything was like it was before. Look, did you threaten Liz or something? Trying to figure out why she disappeared. You were really rude to her you know. I lost my husband and you insulting my best friend. It's not easy for me either you know.'

'I'm sorry Anne. We need to find Liz and I can apologise to her. She never phoned you at all. That's weird. She must be pretty worried. You don't know what happened with her and Stuart do you?' he leaned forward casually pouring another glass of wine.

'What do you mean?' said Anne lowering her gaze.

'Thought Stuart might have mentioned it to you, or even Liz herself. Stuart heard her shagging some guy on his bed- that's when the problems all started. He couldn't bring himself to confront her about it, but after that he barely talked to her and she responded the same way. When she disappeared I even thought Stuart might have harmed her for a while, but she was safe, he found out.'

'Willie, I have to tell you. It was not Liz. It was me. I know the very day it happened.'

Ware remained motionless save a look of bemusement spreading across his face and just stared ahead as Anne continued.

'...it was when I found a note from this Frank guy to Ian and had seen them outside Tennents. I was upset- wanted revenge. I met a guy at the Doublet and we ended up going to Liz's place. Willie, it was me Stuart heard, not her. I told this to Sam Morris already, so I'm sure Stuart knows now. It was the exact time they started not talking and having problems. Liz did nothing. Obviously Stuart has not mentioned it to you yet. She loved Stuart completely and would never have done that. I thought you knew her well enough.'

Ware was flabbergasted. He had been so angered by Liz's apparent infidelity that he had even thought of killing her. The idea suddenly seemed ludicrous. He would have killed an innocent woman in vengeance for hurting the man he loved. He thought of the caravan- if Liz had been still there, he would have killed her for sure. He shuddered. And he had thought of getting rid of Anne too because she might have told Stuart she was gay. It did not seem to matter so much now. Liz and Stuart would get back together regardless and he would be forgotten. He slumped in his chair. His world had changed in an instant. 'But Stuart will be ok- that was the main thing,' he tried only half successfully to convince himself. 'When you love someone, let them go…'

He forced himself upright. 'Anne, you don't know how good that news is to me. Ok, time to tell you. I think I am gay as you said. I hate the very idea. In fact I loathe myself…'

'Why,' said Anne. 'It's no big deal. No one is going to be bothered by it,' she almost laughed.

'You don't understand. For me it is a big deal. When I was fourteen my father started calling me a useless poof, day after fucking day. I could see I had hurt him and denied it to myself. I continued denying it, acting the big tough guy. Then my Mum left. Leaving me with him. It got worse. I was relieved to escape to Uni when I was 18. I never contacted him again. I first met Stuart around that time. I stopped a fight he was part of in Argyle street and we started talking. His Dad sounded even worse than mine, but I could see he was crying out for help. Anyway, I helped him and fell in love with him and still am, but I couldn't admit it to myself, or to him. Even after my father died, I couldn't come out. I have lived a life of quiet desperation as they say. So…I'll admit it to you, but don't tell anyone. I was so enraged about Liz shagging someone in Stuart's bed that I wanted to harm her for hurting

Stuart so much- I traced her in the Highlands, even found out where she was staying and I think I would have killed her if she had been still there, but she left… Maybe even in the back of my mind I was hoping that Stuart and I could be together after, even if it was in a plutonic way, I'd still be happy. It's hard to explain it all. I'm just a fucked up wee poof, I suppose…' He downed the rest of his wine, poured another glass and drank most of that in a one go. 'But I feel happy now. Stuart will know and he will get back with Liz and all will be fine. The main thing is I want him to be happy, that's all. If not with me its ok. Can you understand that? He started to cry. 'I had better go Anne, I'm a wreck.' He said rubbing his eyes and laughing. 'I'm happy, really.'

Anne had been watching and listening carefully. She went over to him and patted him on the arm. 'It will be ok. All will be sorted out soon,' she said.

'Anne, I'm sorry, I'm really sorry. I slept with Ian… it just happened. He was upset with Frank Liddle and…'

Anne jumped mentally at the two new pieces of information her momentary empathy vanished as quickly as it had earlier appeared.

'You slept with Ian? Jesus, my husband- how could you? When was this, once, or more?'

'Once, the night he died. He was at my place just before. I'm sorry Anne…'Ware mumbled.

'Well, fuck you for that. You just said you had talked-you never said he was actually there...' She let it pass for the moment- there was another important matter to discuss.

'This Frank - you know his name, his full name. Liddle? Ian told you about him? What else did he say?' Her voice was stern she realised. Inside her fury was rising quickly. In front of her was a man who had slept with her husband and had admitted that he had been planning to kill her best friend. She felt an urge to take the knife from behind the cushion and stick in right into his bastard heart. She calmed herself as best she could. There was still information to find out, but her mind was frantically planning as she spoke.

'Frank Liddle was it you said. Are you sure?' she asked eagerly.

'Does it matter that much what his name bloody was? said Ware.

'Of course it maters you idiot. I want to know the fucker who ruined my life and find the cunt,' she thought, but said nothing.

Ware continued. 'I remember it a hundred per cent as he was upset with Liddle and mentioned his name several times. I remember it because it sounded like the Supermarket. It was clear Ian was feeling guilty about the affair. In between times he told me not to tell anyone, as Frank was a big shot business man. So, he didn't tell you when you confronted him?'

'No- I knew his first name only.' Said Anne. She now had the name. Ian was dead. Ware was the only other one who had the name. She was planning ahead. She would find this Frank Liddle Mr Big shot and deal with him. First Ware had to be dealt with, this man who new Franks's identity and would remember that he had told Anne if ever asked - and worse- this creature who had been intimate with her husband and had wanted to kill her best friend.

As Ware continued to drink, Anne reached for the knife, then stopped. She would not get away with it. A hundred possibilities raced through her mind. Then one of them settled. She had decided. Her heart was racing…

They sat in silence for a few minutes more and Anne watched him drink two more glasses of wine. He was smashed. 'Good.' thought Anne. 'Helps'.

Ware was crying intermittently while drinking. Anne tried to remain sympathetic in tone when she spoke.

'Willie thanks for coming and I appreciate the truth. It is always good to know everything. I admire you for it and don't worry about Ian, it just happened and we had already broken up…'

'Ian, I'm not worried about *him*. I'm happy. Stuart will be happy when Liz comes back when they find her and that makes me happy, but sad too sort off. I'm a mess I'm afraid.' He reached for another drink, but spilled the wine on the carpet. 'Oh shite,' he muttered.

'Let's get you a taxi.' She said standing up quickly. Inside Ware's words were echoing and getting louder and louder. 'Ian, I'm not worried about *him*.' 'You fucking wanker,' she thought- any doubts in her mind now vanquished.

She called the taxi. It would be there in ten minutes and she would get a call when it arrived. Ware stood up as best he could, but stumbled. 'He's drunk enough,' Anne thought as he tried to regain his balance.

A few minutes later she got the call saying that the taxi was out the door waiting.

'It's here, come on Willie let's get you home.' She took his arm and ushered him towards the door.

'Thanks Anne. I'm pissed I'm afraid. Sorry…really sorry about the carpet.'

'That's ok,' she said. 'Accidents happen…' she opened the door and they moved towards the top of the stairs. She positioned herself behind him, her left arm around the top of his waist, her right leg in front of his ankles. He moved towards the first step. His body was swaying and his foot got caught behind Anne's right leg as she shoved him forward…

'Oops,' he said as he missed the first step and pitched forward…

Professor William Ware was declared dead on arrival at the hospital. A taxi had rushed him there with Anne, but the head injury he had suffered when falling down the stairs had killed him instantly the initial prognosis suggested. Anne had said he had been drunk and she was trying to help him down the stairs but he had stumbled and being such a big man her attempts to hold him back had been in vain. She had run out to the street and asked the waiting taxi to take them to the hospital. Ware's alcohol count when his blood was examined was sky high and there being no other suspicious circumstances the death was quickly recorded as a tragic accident the like of which Glasgow saw many of every year. Anne had told first Stuart and then Morris the day after having given a statement before returning home. Stuart took it badly. His wife was still missing and now both his best pals were dead. Anne had told him nothing of Peter's confessions. Peter's sister from Aberdeen came down to organise the funeral. Anne dressed in black, sat quietly with Stuart and comforted him when they attended. He gave an elegant eulogy mentioning how long they had been friends and how much Ware had done to help and support him before this tragic accident ended his life too soon. Anne sat there nodding slowly and her eyes were fixed in thought. However, she was not recalling memories of times with Ware and especially the last moment of his life. She was now concentrating now on another man. Mr Frank Liddle. Business man and casino owner she had found out after a Google search. She had the guy. His turn to pay…

CHAPTER 14

Morris stood at the top of the street and took in the surrounds. Julia's house was five down on the left. Any movements in and out could be nicely observed from where he was now standing. At the end of the street, a further two houses down from Julia's place, there was a junction and he could see some shops across the adjoining road. Morris had his analytical cap on. 'So, unless the killer knew where Gary Scott lived and followed him when he left for Julia's place, he must have seen him from either here or at the other end of the street. Here is more concealed. If the killer had followed Gary from his flat in Park Road he would have had to stop of and buy the same clothes. So, it was more likely that the killer knew Julia's address and waited for Scott here? 'Yes' he answered himself.

'Ok, but how long did he wait? Possibly he knew what time Gary was coming for his date…maybes yes maybes no…' He looked around for possible vantage points where the killer may have waited for Gary to show up. A wide oak tree behind him stood out as a strong possibility. Morris went over to it. The rain had made the ground around it boggy and dirty, but there on the ground behind the tree were about half a dozen cigarette butts. He went down on one knee and peered at them. All the same brand looked like, judging by the markings on the butts.

'Bingo,' said Morris to himself, thinking of no other reason why someone would stand behind a tree for what was obviously a considerable amount of time unless they were waiting for someone, or watching something. He peered down closely around the cigarette butts. No shoe prints, but maybe the cigarettes would be all he needed. He did not have anything that could be used as a bag on him. He patted himself down and in one of his pockets he found an old, half used packet of Polos. Discarding the sweets, he took a leaf and carefully picked up each cigarette with it and placed it gently into the foil of the Polo wrapping and placed it in his back pocket. 'Could be an excellent start,' he said wishfully, heading into Julia's street. He strolled around, going over the time line of the murder and trying to work out the specifics of how it was done. He was the murderer in his mind.

Eventually a movement caught his eye. It came from the door of the last house on the street before the junction. A man was leaving his house and moving toward the junction. Morris called after him and waved his hand. The man stopped and waited as Morris came towards him.

'Hello, thank you,' Morris started. 'I'm sorry to bother you. Can you spare a moment?'

'What's it about?' Asked the man in curiosity. 'I'm in a wee bit of a hurry…'

'If you could.,. Sam Morris, I'm a friend of Gary Scott…'

The stranger looked at Morris, with some alarm. 'James Bone. Ah, the guy charged with Julia's murder? I have already talked to the police about Julia and what I saw. Not really much more to say. I nearly hit him and saw the blood on his hands and gave a description to them, that's all I know.'

'Oh, you were the actual driver. That's great. Glad to meet you. Must have been a shock. The police are widening their enquiries now, I heard. It's possible they think it may not have been Gary. Maybe someone just happened to be dressed the same…'

'Well, that is interesting. The police were sure it was him. The clothes and the umbrella matched perfectly, but they never really asked me about his face at all. I didn't get too much of a look because he had his umbrella up, but as I remember it the face was not the same as Gary Scott's photo in the news.'

'That's interesting,' said Morris. 'Didn't know about that.'

'I did tell the police of my doubts, but they said I probably didn't get a good look and there was no way a random stranger could be wearing the exact same clothes and carrying the same umbrella. And another thing, I didn't tell the police this one- the guy looked younger. This Scott is seventy, news said. The way the guy moved over the street- his movement- didn't look like someone so old. Fifty-five, sixty, about more like. Was thinking of telling the police that too, but as I said they seem to be sure they have the right guy.'

Morris smiled. It was going well today.

'Things have changed,' he said. 'I can't tell you officially, but I know the police are getting more convinced Gary did not kill Julia. He was here alright and admits that of course, but it looks like he was not involved in the murder- someone was trying to set him up.'

'I see, I see. That's a shocker,' replied the man excitedly. 'Someone must have dressed up like Gary, then…Wow. I had better tell the police straight after I get back from the shops- wouldn't like the wrong guy to be put away. Poor Julia, she was a nice old dear. What a way to go. If it wasn't this Scott guy, I hope they find the killer.'

'Aye, that would be good,' Morris said. 'Fair bit of work to do yet though, but I'm hoping Gary will be released soon. Did you ever talk to Julia? Seems a nice lady. Lived alone I think?'

'She was lovely yes. Had had an interesting life, but think she was struggling for money lately. She had borrowed from a few of us in the last few weeks. Her kids did not contact her much and she was a bit sad about that, but she always gave me a nice smile when I saw her in the street. Lived alone, yes, but I think she did have a boyfriend, although none of us ever saw anyone go into her house except her friend and her daughter once in a blue moon.'

'So she visited the boyfriend you think, rather than him coming here?'

'Well that's what we all think. Mrs Cafferty lives opposite- away on holiday at the moment though.' he pointed over the street to the house on the corner, 'She says she often saw Julia drive into the street in her Mercedes really early in the morning, before six. She is a cleaner so works early shifts so is up at that time, but we think Julia was trying to sneak home before any of the neighbours saw her. She had a Mercedes, so it was definitely her.' Obviously enjoying passing on the gossip Morris thought as the man leaned in a bit closer.

'Except the one time Mrs Cafferty saw Julia being dropped off at the corner a little later around seven and walking up the street from there. It was an even better car. A Rolls! No riff raff for Julia,' said the man starting to laugh and then thinking better off it. 'We will miss her- look- got to go –I'll contact the police in a bit- don't worry.' With that he turned and headed to the junction a few meters away.

'Don't worry,' thought Morris. 'you will soon find someone else to spy on...' but he turned back to walk towards his car, more seeds were being planted and more dots being joined. Once he had got in, he phoned Frazer and told him about what he had been told by Julia's neighbour and the Winston fags he had noticed and gathered up and was on his way to deliver.

Three days later Sam Morris had just got up. He had spoken to Linda the night before and there was an offer for her house which she said she had accepted. She reckoned she would move down to Glasgow in about three weeks. Morris felt the warm glow of anticipation. Things had worked out well with her. As the kettle boiled for his coffee, the phone went. It was Frazer.

'Morning Sam,' he said. 'All Good?'

'Fine thanks. You?'

'Good news. Forensics managed to get a DNA extract from the fags. We are lucky. It's hard to get extracts with all the inhibiting junk they put into cigarettes, but we got a match. Confirmed Winston- all of them. Even better is that we got a match on the smoker.'

'What? Great. That was quick. Some criminal I'll bet then. Any previous?'

'Can't tell you more just now. Just to tell you that we will find him and bring him in for a wee chat. It's a long way to go from him standing behind a tree smoking fags to proving that he later went into Julia's place and committed murder, but we will do our best. The driver might be able to recognize him – so there is a chance there too. Working flat out to get any more evidence. Initial feeling is that this time I think we have the right bloke.'

'Ok, good news looks like. I'm very curious to see who it is, but I can wait. Understand you can't say just now. Ok pal, thanks for the call- kettle's boiling…

On the same day as Ware's funeral, Gary Scott was released from police custody. He received a personal apology from Frazer and was offered a lift to his house which he accepted. He collected Rory from the neighbour who had been looking after him, took him a quick walk, stopped off at an ATM machine, got some fish fingers for his dinner and headed straight to the Doublet. He felt great- vindicated. He opened the door dramatically. The seven drinkers inside glanced up automatically.

'I'm back! Mass Murderer released from prison. Barman a pint of your finest ale sir. Accompanied by a Malt of the Month if you please. In fact, drinks all round. It's not very day you get released from prison for attempted murder.' He saw Burns was in, gesticulating and talking to a bemused newcomer. He smiled remembering it was Phil's remarks about jealousy that had made him remember Julia and end up with him being arrested for her murder, but he certainly had no hard feelings towards him, or anyone else at this moment. Morris was there too. He was going to enjoy today. He turned to Burns who was gleefully accepting the free pint being poured for him.

'Phil, my friend,' he said raising his pint in greeting. 'I have a question for you. To get fu, or not to get fu- that is the question? What's the answer pal?'

Straight faced, Burns replied in mock pomposity.

'I prefer the former course of action when this difficult conundrum is presented to me.' They both stopped for a second then burst out laughing. 'That is good news Phil, for you and I are going to get well pished today and tonight and tomorrow at lunchtime.'

'I'm in,' laughed Burns.

Morris was sitting on his usual chair. He looked up and smiled at the beaming Scott. Scott had been unaware of Morris' involvement but when their eyes met they both raised their pints in salutation. 'The truth will out,' Morris thought. 'Well, we know half the truth now, a criminal match for the cigarettes and the police will hopefully get something from the diary, or follow up and try and trace that Rolls, so it's not quite finished yet- but he had done his part. His friend Gary Scott was uninvolved and free. 'Good stuff.' He called over to Gary as a Guinness was placed on his table. 'Here's to your good health man. Thanks for the pint,' he called over to where Scott and Burns were standing.

CHAPTER 15

Frank Liddle, tall, smoothly combed black hair and well dressed in suit and tie, sat in his office in the Casino he owned in Sauchiehall street. Business there was ok, nothing great. The Casino was more of an interest, a side line now. By buying a casino and seeing how it operated he could develop his main business. He had been a bookmaker and had then recently moved into on line Gambling using live feeds from Casinos in the north of Cyprus, Malta and Romania. He used good looking boys and attractive girls with low cut dresses who dealt roulette and the on line punters could bet freely, if illegally, as they wanted with limits determined by his Managers at the scene. Liddle left his office and walked around the casino. Wednesday night. There were about ten people in. Three playing Black Jack, two on Poker, one lady on Electronic Roulette and four on the two opened Roulette tables. He looked at the roulette as the dealer spun the ball. The House advantage was a reasonable

2.7%. it did not sound too much, but in theory that was amount of profit he would get for every bet placed. On a thousand pounds bet his return was 27 quid. He watched the roulette players placing their bets and did some quick mental calculations. It was small scale, but paid the bills along with the other games. He remembered the Turkish guy who had asked to meet him and tried to sell the on line live game business. They wanted his name to front the company to give it respectability. It would be registered as a casino consulting company in Malta, but the actual operations would be illegal. Liddle had no problem with that. Abiding by the law was not a priority for him.

'The great thing is the punters see the actual game,' the Turkish guy had said enthusiastically. 'If there is no actual live - just a generated winning number, there is always the suspicion that the numbers are fixed so that the on line casino wins more. When they see a real game with their own eyes, the trust is much more and the betting levels shoot up. Add to that the excitement and it's a much better alternative. Let me put it like this. In a physical casino you might have six or seven players around a Roulette table. Our place in Cyprus has had six thousand on line players playing at the same time. Think of that. The maths… Six thousand bets per spin. Average bet we have is twenty Euro. On hundred and twenty thousand bet every spin. Three grand in your pocket per spin. And with so many players all the numbers are generally covered equally on line, so volatility is minimal,'

Liddell had not really understood the last part, but he heard the numbers and it was clear that this was a fantastic opportunity. He did his research and eventually joined up with the holding company the seller had represented – 'Horizon'- opening a new live game on line business with them in Cyprus, but registered as 'Horizon Consulting' in Malta. The Gaming operations being called, 'Let's Play' He had kept a keen eye on the numbers as they had come in after the opening. Average players were ten thousand a day playing thirty-two spins each with an average of two thousand bettors between midnight and two in the morning. Average bet was fifteen Euros per spin and spins per day from opening at two in the afternoon to six in the morning were seven hundred and twenty. They had started with five roulette tables and now had eight, with plans for four more being considered. The company paid the staff very well and tax was non-existent. To ensure money was transferred quickly, the day's wins and very occasional losses were transferred from and paid into Horizons central Gaming account immediately on the closing of the Gaming day. The Turkish agent had made that crystal clear, saying there could be no exceptions, or delay. As Liddle returned to his office he concluded with satisfaction that it was the best move he ever made. The worst had been getting involved with his previous lover Ian Smith. He had met him here at the bar. Smith came in for a late night drink and they got talking. Liddle could see he was drunk and found him attractive. He was some mixed up guy though. Eventually he saw the attraction was mutual. They had gone back to Frank's place that night and then after sex, Ian had left in the early hours, worried about his wife. On reading that Ian Smith had been killed in a hit and run accident he had shrugged it off. He had seen Ian a few times after that first time but the attraction for him soon waned and he was in the process of ending the relationship anyway. Smith's death had meant nothing much to him. He had a new lover now. John. A much more sensible boy. 'Time for a wee drink,' he concluded, opening the drinks cabinet and pouring himself a brandy. He was unaware that outside his office, Anne Smith had entered the casino

CHAPTER 16

There had been an extended article in the Herald about the death of Professor William Ware several days after his death. He was well known in the academic world and the article was longer than the usual obituary. It mentioned 'close friend' Anne Smith who had rushed him to the hospital in vain. 'Tragic accident.' Still stuck in her Hotel room, Liz Hislop had read it in shock, but after, with some relief. A lot of relief. He had been looking to harm her. Now he was dead. Was it safe to go back home? Could be. Stuart? And poor Anne. Her husband dead and now a close friend of her and Ian's. She sat on her bed. She had already decided to check out and find a cheaper place just before she had seen the newspaper article. But now she felt different. Hope rose in her. Ware- the principle reason for her flight - was dead. She had thought about it for a few days, but now made up her mind and picked up the phone. It now seemed safe enough. She called her best friend.

'Anne, it's me, Liz.'

"Liz, Liz,' Anne found herself shouting down the phone. 'Hold on a minute, I'm in a shop, let me get outside.'

When she was outside she continued. 'Oh My God. I was worried sick. Even when I heard you were ok, I was still praying you would call me and explain. It wasn't just me- everyone was worried. Are you ok, where are you?'

'I'm fine Anne. I am in the Hilton would you believe. I read about Willie's death. What happened?'

'It was terrible,' Anne said. 'I was with him at my place. He got terribly drunk and fell down the steps and smashed his head and died instantly. Awful. Poor man…Stuart and I went to the funeral Anyway- we have so much to talk about…'

'Listen Anne, I want to apologise straight away. You must hate me for not contacting you,' said Liz.

'No, well, yes, I was a wee bit angry- more like upset. Why did you just go like that?'

'I had to. It was weird. Ian sent me…'

'Ian?'

'Yes, Ian. I'm so sorry for you for his death Anne. It must have just been not long before- he sent me a message warning me that I had to get away, that Willie, as I guessed, was maybe going to harm me. He also told me not to tell anyone. I was a bit shocked, but probably would not have done anything. Then I found an awful note in my bag, then you told me Ian had been killed. It was coming at me from all sides-all at once. After that I panicked. I thought I might be next. I did not know where to go. I ended up escaping up north and staying in a caravan. I took Ian's advice and did not contact anyone- even you. I had no idea of what was going on, but I was terrified. I just packed up a few things and left. I did phone and met Quita in town- that was silly – I barely spoke to her- but she did not know Willie well, so that must have been what made me contact her, as a sort of desperate last contact. I was already on my way back to Glasgow- I reckoned staying in a hotel would be safer- when I saw Willie in Ullapool, so that made me even more paranoid. Maybe he wasn't, but in my fear, I was sure he was looking for me - to harm me. I'm in the Hilton now- its cost me a fortune too.'

Anne spoke. 'Wow, I understand a bit now. Just before Willie fell down the steps he told me Ian had been at his place just before his death and you are right- he did plan to harm you. He said he found where you were staying up north and would have killed you he said, but you had left. And we were right about thinking he was gay- he admitted it and he…' she stopped, finding she could not tell Liz that Ian had slept with Ware. 'Anyway, don't know if I would have done the same as you and just left, but I see where you are coming from. Stuart though- couldn't you leave a message at least. He thought you might be dead. And now Willie is dead too. Awful as that is, it surely means you can come home now if he was the one you were scared of. That's if you trust Stuart...Liz, I can't really bring myself to say it just now and when you find out please don't hate me for it, but you will find Stuart will welcome you with open arms. I know we talked about something that had driven him to be nasty to you- well, it's clear now- he had the wrong information. He will explain- trust me- you will be fine with him… maybe not with me…'

'Whatever it is, that's great to hear. So he had the wrong reason to hate me? Well I'll give him a good telling to!' she laughed down the phone. Anne did not reciprocate. Not only did Liz feel safe to go home, it now looked like she would be even be welcome there. After the last nightmarish few weeks' things seemed to be looking up.

They talked a bit more- arranged to meet for lunch and finishing the call, Liz took a deep breath and phoned Stuart. He quickly told her about the reason for his animosity towards her apologizing every few seconds while he did so. Her anger at him believing she would even do that was overcome by her desire to see him again and her home again. As Anne had indicated and after the initial shock and hesitancy and mutual apologies-for not trusting each other – he asked her to return and she accepted without a moment's hesitation. They would discuss the whole thing over a dinner he would prepare. Liz excitedly packed, paid the bill and half an hour later was back at the front door of their home. Stuart rushed to the door as he heard her coming up the stairs. He remembered the sound of her heels just before she had left. Now she was walking not away, but back into his life. He opened the door and they remained silent for a moment before collapsing into each other's arms. This was their first embrace in over two months and each lingered, wanting to take in and remember the moment. 'Baby, I'm so sorry,' he whispered. She pushed him back lightly. 'And so you damn well should be. Now run me a bath and wait in our bedroom…You will receive your punishment anon,' she winked, too happy to blame him for his mistrust. Stuart's grin stretched through his beard, as he moved quickly towards the bathroom.

CHAPTER 17

A week later Ronald 'Ringo' Dunn sat facing Frazer in the interview room. He had been identified after the DNA extracted from two of the cigarettes had been run through the data base and matched his records from a long and varied criminal career. Once the police had finished their further enquiries he had been located at his last known address and brought in to Dumbarton road police station. He was looking sunburnt and was dressed in a plain white T shirt and blue slacks. It was obvious he had been away on holiday- he certainly hadn't got that colour sunbathing on Glasgow Green. Dunn looked relaxed to Frazer. He remembered Gary Scott's bewilderment in contrast. He had got it wrong initially with him, so reminded himself to have no presumptions with this suspect, but he had the evidence in front of him.

'Mr Dunn- may I call you Ronald?' he started.

'Ringo is fine,' came the smiling reply.

'No thanks Ronald, I'll stick with that. Right. You were briefed about why you were here, so let's find out what you know about Julia Sinclair. You knew her, from where Ronald?'

Dunn put a surprised look on his face. 'Never met her before Sir. Something obviously wrong in your Investigation methods, I'm afraid. Won't be the first time they have hauled me in when they can't find the right guy. 'Let's just get a known criminal and blame him'- looks like to me. So voila- here I am. You already screwed up once with the other guy you tried to blame for it. Go ahead, try your best.'

'Cocky wee cunt,' Frazer thought, but his face remained passive. 'We will, believe me,' Frazer smiled.

'Can you tell me why you were standing behind a tree at the top of the street where Julia Sinclair lived Ronald?' Frazer asked.

'What street, I saw her address in the news, but have no idea where it is. I wasn't behind any tree. That's rubbish.'

'Do you smoke Winston fags?' Frazer asked, looking intently for any flicker of reaction.

He saw it. A moment's stopping of body movement- a tiny widening of the eyes.

'Been following me around, or something,' Dunn said a little too quickly, thinking someone must have seen him behind the tree. He had seen no one looking at him, he was sure. 'Keep calm,' he reminded himself. 'If that's all they have it's a doddle.'

'No we didn't follow you around Ronald. You were daft enough to leave your cigarette butts behind a tree and since it's a little unusual to find eight cigarettes behind a tree all the same brand we had a look for DNA and Bingo, Ringo, we found yours there.'

Inside Dunn's heart was racing, he had to be quick. 'That's amazing since I wasn't there. You know DNA can be wrong anyway, so I'm afraid this time it must be a mistake.'

'Oh, but Ronald, that's not all we have. We showed your picture to the driver of the car that nearly ran over Julia's' killer and guess what, he says he caught enough of a glimpse of your face to believe that it could be you who he saw running across the road.'

'Could be' did you say? Must be wrong again pal,' said Dunn, but Frazer could detect a slight tremble in the tone of his reply. 'Now for the knockout punch…' he thought.

'But he was not the only one who recognized you Ronald. We went around the shops and asked. You see it was baffling to us, how it was that you were dressed exactly the same way as Gary. Then we figured it out Ronald. Quite clever I'll give you that, but the best plans go aft agaly….as it has in this case. When did you come up with that plan- once he arrived in the street? When you watched him go into the house while smoking your Winstons? Anyway, you figured you could dress up like him, kill Julia and Gary would get the blame. Good idea, but maybe you should have gone shopping a bit further afield. You just went to Mayhill road and visited a few charity shops. Got you on CCTV pal. We also found that your bank account got a sudden credit of twelve thousand pounds the day before Julia was killed and the same two days after -plenty for a wee holiday looks like. That's a very interesting coincidence too. We know you have done fire insurance jobs for people in the past and we are just wondering about this one. Murder a bit of a step up Ronald, even for a career criminal like yourself. The only question we need to know - and think carefully before you answer Ronald because it could make a huge difference in how long you are sent down for- is why she was killed and who did the ordering?'

Dunn tried one last throw of the dice. 'Aye you are right- sorry I forgot. I did do some shopping in that area recently, but it's just a coincidence that I bought the same clothes. The money was won at a casino. Two good wins. Anyway, after shopping I went to a pub and stayed till closing. I never went near her house. You can check the pub out. The Wee Slope. So you see, it could not have been me. Sorry old chap.'

Frazer stared straight into Dunn's eyes. He was lying- Frazer knew it, but he just had to check this pub story out first. He ended the interview, Dunn was returned to his holding cell and Frazer immediately arranged for The Wee Slope to be visited to see if Burns claimed visit could be verified. He got the results two hours later. The initial report confirmed that the barman, Billy Steele, had remembered him and the date because he remembered it was the time when Sinclair had been killed in the neighborhood. Frazer had cursed but insisted on a full statement form the barman. The next day Frazer got the results of the follow up. The barman had recalled that Dunn had gone out for half an hour to find an ATM and get some fags. He had remembered where Dunn had said he had gone- the co-op and a ATM. They had the time, date and location. CCTV review showed Dunn was never there. Frazer had slammed his fist on his office table on getting confirmation. Even better, the pub's CCTV had showed Dunn leaving the pub quickly and heading towards Julia's street less than ten minutes before the killer had been seen entering her house. He must have had 'Scott's' clothes stashed and changed into them quickly beforehand. 'Shouldn't have forgot the cameras Ronald,' Frazer had smiled to himself.

The next day Dunn was back in the interview room. Frazer dismantled the alibi in front of him and he visibly wilted as it was related. Frazer said. 'Excuse my language, but you are fucked Ronald. Master Criminal you are most definitely not. I'll ask you one more time. Why was she killed and who ordered it?

Does he drive a Rolls per chance?' Dunn slumped in his chair, thought for a minute looked around the room in desperation and then started to tell Frazer the whole story. On checking Julia Sinclair's address book, they got a match on Colin Worth's phone number under an abbreviated entry 'C.W. (Bastard).'

Colin Worth had heard that Ringo had been picked up. Getting a message to him to threaten, or promise him the earth to keep him out of it, had proved impossible. Ringo had no family- so that route of intimidation was not open either. Worth had decided to make a run for it. He transferred a large sum to an account in Switzerland, flew over to France and was collected at Charles de Gaulle by an associate. He then moved around Europe before taking a ferry to Jersey two weeks later. It would be three months later when we would be tracked down and arrested and deported to Glasgow to face trial for the murder of Julia Sinclair along with Ronald Dunn. Worth would express no regret as he was led down to commence his life long prison sentence. At sixty-eight years old he knew he would never be released. His kids had disowned him. He had nothing left. Just one mission remained set in his mind. To find where Dunn would be held and arrange for him to be killed. It would take a while, but Ronald Dunn would be found dead in his cell two weeks later. He had been strangled and slashed from ear to ear with a sharpened screwdriver.

CHAPTER 18

Since their friend Ian had been involved, Stuart and Liz Hislop had followed the Sinclair murder case avidly. So too had Anne Smith. Her husband had been killed by Julia Sinclair, but she bore her no malice. It had been an accident. But the man who had taken Ian away from her- that was a different story. He had to pay, as Ware had done. She was in the casino that Liddle owned in Sauchiehall street, but kept a low profile and did not ask any questions to either the staff, or customers. She did however, see someone entering and leaving an office who was a match for Liddle's LinkedIn profile photo. She looked at him closely. Remembering the details of his face and body – the body her husband had shared. The only question now was how? Ware had been a doddle. She hoped Frank could be disposed of with equal ease. She felt calm. She wanted him to die. It was her right to avenge her loss. Of that she was in no doubt. She knew people would judge her differently if they found out, but they did not understand the betrayal she had gone through and her sense of helplessness and hatred. Not once, but twice- her own infidelity justified in her own mind. She just had to get the plan right. An idea was already forming. Just setting it up would be hard. She played Slots keeping an eye on the office and Liddle's movements when he came and went from it. At two in the morning she saw something interesting. A young waiter was ushered into the office by Liddle and there was a look shared between them and Liddle briefly ran his hand down the waiter's arm. At three they both reappeared with Liddle holding a briefcase and the waiter had changed put of his uniform. Liddle went to the cash desk and looked at some documents and the cashiers screen and then turned and walked towards the exit with the young lad in tow behind. Liddle nodded to a few people on the way put and shook hands with a couple of customers. He looked happy and relaxed, the young boy less so. He was only about twenty-one. Anne followed them discretely on the way out, watched them get into a car. The same car she had seen Ian get into outside Tennents pub on Byres road. As the car pulled out she quickly got into her own car and followed. The car headed up to the West End along Woodlands road and up to University Avenue over to Byres road. The irony was not lost on Anne. The car was passing the very spot where Ian had been run over by Sinclair and killed.

She wondered if Ian's lover driving the car with the young boy by his side gave it a moment's thought. She hated him with all her heart she realised. She was still level headed enough to fear being caught. She wanted revenge, but had no desire to end her days in prison. She needed a water tight plan and alibi. She thought of how Ian's killer had only been caught by luck, with Gary Scott remembering Julia in the car. Otherwise, she would probably have never been caught. Could she pull off the same- using the same way? She followed Liddle as he drove up to Hynland. When she saw he was slowing down to stop outside a house she drew in behind a car and out of sight and watched. The young lad and Liddle went into a large house holding hands and obviously chatting. Anne thought of waiting to see when the lad would leave but presuming he was probably there for the night, reversed and headed home. She got back to her place and had a shower - planning all the time. She went straight to bed after drying off. She was meeting Liz for lunch and needed some sleep.

It was Frank's young lover, John Manning, who had noticed Anne's car following. As they had pulled out from the Casino at two thirty Sauchiehall street was quiet and he had seen, but rarely registered Anne walking quickly and getting into her own car. By the time they neared Hynland, he was pretty sure that he and Frank were being followed. He was unsure if he should say anything. Normally he was expected to shut up and say little, but he wanted to impress Frank. He knew a man in his position would have enemies. When they turned into Franks street he glanced in the rearview mirror and saw Anne's car pull in behind another car at the end of the road. He turned to face Frank.

'There has been someone following us since we left the casino. I'm sure.' Liddle was involved in enough illegal activities and with dangerous associates to take any such suspicions seriously.

'Are you sure? Did you get a sight of him? How many were in the car?'

'It was a woman actually. Just her and quite old…'

Liddle laughed,' A new breed of deadly assassins.' He turned to the boy and squeezed his hands. 'It's ok John. I'm sure nothing to worry about. But thanks.' They got out the car and Liddle laughed about it as they walked up the path to his door. Later that night he got up, visited the toilet and poured a small brandy sitting down in the lounge next to the fireplace and thinking. The boy had said they had been followed from the Casino. 'Fuck it,' he said softly and made a call to the Surveillance department asking them to ID the women and inform of any interesting information they had on her.

'Be quick,' he ordered, 'I want to get back to bed.' Eight minutes later he got the call.

'Mr Liddle. Sorry, we were as quick as we could be. Got the ID. Lady who got into the car came out the casino a minute after you and John. Got into her car and followed your direction up Sauchiehall…'

'I know that but, what's her name? Background?' He asked impatiently.

'Anne Smith.'

'Never heard of her. Never seen her in the casino before either…' Liddell muttered.

'Mr Liddell, there is something interesting. We checked her registration of course. It was her first visit, but the interesting thing was that her registration address was shared with your previous VIP guest…'

'VIP guest, which one'? asked Liddell, becoming slightly more interested.

'Ian Smith- your close friend- the guy who was killed in a Hit and Run by an old lady in the West End a while back. Looks like this Anne Smith was his wife.'

The world seemed to suddenly stop still for Frank Liddell. He ended the call and stared into the embers of the dying out fire. 'Shite. She knows…'

Anne was having lunch with Liz in Ashton Lane. They had a drink and then moved to their table. The tension in the air was palpable.

'Liz, you haven't said anything yet. Did Stuart tell you?'

Liz nodded grimly. 'Yes, he did. More or less immediately after I got back. I'm not too happy that you took a man to my house and to our bed. All the trouble it caused. But to be honest, I can't be bothered hating anyone just…'

Anne interrupted. 'No Liz, it was a bloody awful thing to do. I was more or less reconciled to losing Ian forever, was drunk and wanted to be held…but there really is no excuse. Looking back, I can't believe I did that. And all the problems it ended up causing everyone. Stuart thought you were…'

Liz interrupted. 'I know. I was angry when he told me. A bit with you, but mostly with him – he should have trusted me- but thinking about it I suppose anyone would have come to the same conclusion as he did. He is not great at confronting problems either, not that I'm any better, but if only he had told me there and then, I could probably have figured it was you since no one else has a spare set of keys. Anyway, it's over now. I learnt a bit about myself too while I was away. I'm an awful ditherer!' They shared a forced laugh as their starters arrived. They ate in silence for a while.

'Right.' Anne said. 'Best friends- no secrets. Willie contacted me and we chatted and he came round to my place. He was in a strange mood. Before coming I knew he was lying on the phone, but I wanted to know what he knew about Ian.'

'Right- can imagine,' Liz nodded. 'So, what did he say.' Liz leaned forward interested.

'Well before you disappeared, remember I told you Ian had seen seeing a man. Frank somebody. Willie was well pissed and told me his full name and that he was a big business guy- casino's mostly- that's where Ian had met him. I Googled and found him easy enough. Frank Liddle. I actually followed him home last night'

'This Frank guy? Whatever for?'

'Liz, if you knew how I felt. The bitterness. I saw him in the casino walking around as if nothing happened- bastard- and he had a new lover looks like. Ian dead, forgotten, a ruined marriage- all because of him.'

'Ok, understand the bitterness, but it was not as if he killed Ian- that was that old lady. You know she is dead now?'

'Yes. That was a shame. The hit and run was an accident. I'm sure she didn't mean to harm Ian- this Frank Liddle knew what he was doing though- I can't forgive him for taking advantage of Ian and for hurting me. So I followed him home with his new boyfriend.'

'For God's sake why Anne? You have to forget about it.'

Anne leaned forward and whispered. 'I can't forget about it. I want him hurt. I have even thought of killing him…'

Liz sat upright. 'Eh? Don't be so bloody silly Anne. End up in prison for the rest of your life because Mr Frank whoever slept with your husband and hurt you?

Come on. Maybe Ian did not even tell Frank that he was married. In fact, there is a good chance he didn't I would reckon. Look if you need some sort of closure, confront him, give him a bit of your mind- but that's all for God's sake. You need to get over this. Did you say all this to Willie?'

Anne paused and looked at the wall of the restaurant for a second. 'Willie…oh Willie. I'll tell you something else Willie told me. He and Ian slept together the night I threw him out of the house. He just mentioned it as if it was no big deal. I hated him for that. They slept together and then Ian left to go home and was killed that same night- morning, I mean.'

Liz gasped at the news of Ian and Ware. 'They slept together too. I'm sure that added to your pain. I'm sorry Anne. You got it from all sides. Ian must have just left Willie's house when he sent me the warning message. Something must have happened there for Ian to warn me so forcefully about him. Maybe Willie was worried that Ian would tell me about their sleeping together, but that's no big deal really? Something else…?'

'Willie loved Stuart, Liz…' Anne whispered.

"What? Lifelong friends, but that was all. What the hell are you talking about now Anne?'

'No, no, it wasn't reciprocal. Just complicated. When Stuart told Willie about who he thought was you shagging someone in your bed, he lost it. How you could betray and hurt his love and all that… That's why he had been nasty to you. He was happy you were with Stuart because he could see Stuart was happy, but when it seemed you had betrayed him and hurt him Ware flipped. You were wise to run away, it probably saved your life. He was in a right mess at the flat,'

'Phew,' said Liz. 'A lot to take in. So he told you all this and fell down the steps. If you were so angry with this Frank guy for sleeping with your husband, why weren't you so bothered about Willie doing it with him…'

Then she stopped. Her eyes fixed on Anne's and they starred at each other for several seconds. 'Anne… you didn't…?'

Anne quickly diverted her eyes. 'When he told me that, I was furious I'll admit. The way he just dismissed it as a nothing. We got to the top of the stairs when I called a taxi – I wanted him out of the house the minute he told me- but then he was so drunk he tripped at the top of the stairs. I tried to grab him, but he was so big. He was dead when we got the hospital. But I hated him then and still do- I'll tell you that. She looked at Liz directly again. 'We are best friends Liz, so it's just between us, ok.'

'Ok. Willie was an accident but if something non accidental happens to this Frank guy…no way, you can't expect me to say nothing. I'm sure he has friends and family too Anne. So stop talking about getting rid of him you idiot. If you feel you need some sort of closure or some sort of revenge, then confront him or give him a wee scare, but getting rid of him permanently…You might need some help Anne can I say- I can't really understand this ultimate revenge thing. I'll help in any way I can, you know that.' She placed her hand on Anne's shoulder and let it linger there.

Anne shook her head. 'It's just all been too much for me. The rejection I felt – the humiliation- the anger it caused…I can't face him -I could just lose it even if he never knew I was Ian's wife.'

'I know, I know,' said Liz, 'But you need to calm down. Look you said he is a Casino Boss. Why don't you go in take all is money- that will make you feel better?' She said the last comment in a humorous tone intending to lighten up the situation.

Anne laughed a little, thought for a bit and nodded. 'That would be good. I'd love to see his face when he lost everything. Aye, that could do the trick maybe.'

Liz wondered for a second if what she had suggested had been wise, but she saw the look on Anne's face and if she did do something at the casino anything would be better than what she had originally planned for Frank.

'I don't know anything about casinos though,' Anne said ruefully. 'Just put the money in the machines and press a button and hope for the best…'

There was silence for a few seconds and then it seemed to dawn on them at the same time.

'Sam Morris,' they both said.

That evening, after a call to Morris, Anne, Liz and Stuart met him at the Doublet. They had wine and beers and went over the whole story of the Hit and Run and all the characters involved. It was all over now as far as Morris was concerned. He remembered the chaos theory quote about a butterfly beating its wings in Brazil and this leading to a tornado in Texas. It had all been a bit like that. Gary Scott seeing Julia Sinclair in the car who had run over and killed Ian and who had been killed by Ronal Dunn on the orders of Colin Worth and Gary Scott who had been accused of the killing and then freed and now Anne and Liz were telling him about Ian, Ware and Frank Liddle. Morris shook his head and had a large sip of Guinness. Egged on by Liz, Anne told Morris and Stuart about following Frank home and her desire to get some sort of revenge as closure.

'So Anne was thinking of hurting him at the casino somehow,' Liz said.

Morris initially laughed. 'Rob him are you saying. How? You would end up in prison. Not much of a closure there- don't be daft.'

Anne spoke frankly and slowly.

'Sam, I need to be able to close this. It might sound petty to you – I don't expect you to understand, but...'

Morris took her words on board. He remembered his own pettiness with Linda and the hurt it had caused and the feeling when the pain had gone. Crazy as this plan sounded, maybe it was what Anne needed somehow. 'Never try and judge others motives,' he reminded himself yet again.

He raised his hands and spoke. 'Ok, Ok…sorry. But couldn't you just meet him and have it out. That might help -clear it all up?'

Anne shook her head. 'Liz said the same. I don't really trust myself. If he said the wrong thing- dismissed it as trivial, for example- I could just flip. I know I could. No, I want to see him hurt and I want to see his face when that happens- so he knows how I felt- but it's probably best I'm not actually next to him when it happens- for his sake.'

Morris realised they were all looking at him in anticipation. He was pretty sure Stuart had been forewarned about this casino plan that was being fomented. 'What to do?'

After a few seconds he let out a deep breath and spoke. 'Look, you can rip of a casino. In fact, I know just the people if they are still around.'

'The Blitzkrieg Scammers you talked about before.' Said Stuart, sounding a little too excited Morris felt.

'Well yes I suppose. I have not been in contact with Marco Capone since the last scam that happened in South Africa and Vegas- but yes- them.'

'You said that the team of cheats had their hands cut off by one of the big Asian bosses.'

'Six of them, yes. But there was a big team of them then. Dozens to pick from,' said Morris, noticing the look of alarm on Anne and Liz's faces. 'See what you have let yourselves in for.' He laughed to himself, before continuing. 'But look, you can't ask me to get involved in organizing a casino scam. I'm the guy who was supposed to solve them remember.'

Anne jumped in. 'Ok, we know that Sam, but couldn't you just introduce us to that team and maybe we can tempt them to rip off Frank.'

'They are not here Anne. In a place called Tolo in Italy. From what I remember the casino there was taken over by Stanley Ling and is legit now, but look, I'll give you Marco's number and you can contact him. But that's it. I want absolutely nothing more to do with it. That clear? Hundred per cent not involved. This is just to help your mad cap plan- that's me finished.' Morris handed over the number. He felt a little annoyed with himself for even doing that and in a way he hoped Marco would reject any scam proposals. He finished his pint and got up to leave, turning to Anne. 'If you feel you have to do this, fair enough, I sort of understand. But prepare for consequences.' Anne and the others just stared at him as he strode out the Doublet.

Instead of walking home, Morris passed the door of his tenement and crossed over Eldon street and into Kelvingrove Park. He wanted a wee think. He was already annoyed with himself for giving Anne Marco Capone's phone number. 'Me, part of a scam, however small the part?'.' He chided himself. He sighed, 'Bugger it.' He phoned Marco in Italy who answered after the fifth ring, speaking in Italian until he recognised Marris' voice.

'Mr Morris! Ah, a lovely surprise. How are you my friend? I hope no bad news? Every time you called in the past, it was some bad news for me! Everything is ok? Where are you now?'

'Hello Marco. I'm fine thanks and phoning from a park in Glasgow. How is the business? Mr Ling a good boss?

'Ah, Mr Ling. He has never visited,' said Marco. 'But he trusts me enough and we are doing very good. All legitimate now, I may say truthfully to you.'

Morris laughed, but his annoyance with himself was growing.

'Marco, I'll come straight to the point. Have you had another call from Scotland in the last few minutes- a lady called Anne Smith?'

Capone sounded confused. 'No, the last time I got a call from Scotland was from you. No one has called- no lady- anyone. Why- what is the matter? I don't like the sound of your voice.'

'I can't really explain too well but this woman lost her husband- he was killed in a car accident- but he had left her for a man…Anyway, even though this man had nothing to do with the accident, she wants to get revenge on him- make him pay for destroying her marriage. Hell hath no fury sort of thing…Well, she asked for my help. I don't know why really, maybe out of perverse sympathy, but I gave your phone number knowing you guys are the best-or were. After that I told her I did not want anything to do with it, but just now thought I should at least call and you can tell her no yourself. I apologise Marco-it was stupid of me. I feel like I have dropped you in the shit.'

'Nothing from you is ever stupid Sam,' replied Marco. 'But I am a little confused. What has this man got to do with casinos?'

'I didn't say? Sorry. He owns a Casino in Glasgow.'

'Name?'

'Frank Liddle.'

'I know this man! He owns more than a little Casino in Glasgow. He is one of the big live on line owners in conjunction with some very bad Turkish mafia in Cyprus and probably other places.'

'Oh, didn't know that,' replied Morris. 'Don't really follow the on line, or any other casino, news much these days.'

'You should. It is big, big business. Yes, very interesting. I know this man very well. Mr Frank Liddle.'

'Ok. Anyway Marco, I just wanted to inform you that this Anne Smith will probably phone very soon and you can just tell her to forget it. Don't worry, I'm sure she won't kill the guy if you turn her down!' he laughed meekly and was about to end the call.

'Wait, wait Sam. I have a story to tell you. Two of our beautiful girls here went to Cyprus to start work in one of his on line places. They were offered big money. They came back together a week later in tears. One of them, Maria Lambardo was raped by the Turkish Assistant Manager and he hit her too. Oh yes, I know about Mr Frank Liddle and his Turkish friends Sam.'

'That is not good Marco. Poor girl. She went to the police?'

'What do you think? The Turkish police in Northern Cyprus? They would have laughed at her. Think of the money they get in the back pocket. No, she and Bella just found a way to get out of there and returned. Maria is still not recovered- a beautiful girl ruined. When she got back and told us we sent an email to their head Office talking about the behavior of the Assistant Manager, but there has been no reply.'

'So this Frank guy will know about it surely?'

'Yes- and has done nothing. I am very angry too Sam.'

'You want to hit them?' said Morris pondering the possibilities.

'It has crossed my mind. We still have most of the team available'.

Morris was thinking. He had believed Anne's justification for wanting to rip off Frank Liddell was too extreme because he had 'only' taken her husband away and ruined the marriage, but if Marco had a plan to attack Liddle's casino because one of his staff had been raped and beaten, that was entirely justifiable. 'Don't judge people's motivation with your own standards,' he reminded himself. If Anne felt like that, so be it. As a friend of a good friend he should have been willing to help and not have done begrudgingly. He was pleased he had phoned Marco now.

'Well, speaking as someone not directly involved. You said you sent an email and no reply. That means Frank knows about the rape and has done nothing – looks like. As a Surveillance guy I should not say this, but he deserves a little, or a very big lesson.'

'I agree totally Sam. However, as you know our activities have caused us a lot of trouble in the past. We have six boys in the town without their hands. I am worried to try again.'

'Yes- that is a point. These Turkish guys sound very bad. It would be dangerous. What was I thinking…?'

'Hey Mr Morris! Don't give up so quickly. I think I might have a safe way- a better way.'

'Ok, go ahead, sounds interesting…' replied Morris.

'This is what I have been thinking. One of our ex dealers, Roberto, ex Scam team moved to Greece to work. Loutraki- you know it I think?'

'Very well.' Morris confirmed.

'He did not do anything wrong there by the way, but he contacted his brother two days ago and said he was offered a job in Cyprus. It's the same place as Maria and Bella went to work.'

'Didn't his brother know about Maria?'

'Yes, everyone knows in the town. His brother had already told him about that, but Roberto said he would be safe and the money was too good. He is as angry as everyone else about Maria and I was thinking that maybe we could use him for something?'

'As a dealer? Your guys operate on the other side of the table…?'

'Yes, but Roberto has a little talent that is a very good one and I'm sure with a little talking to he can help us get revenge.'

Despite himself Morris was intrigued and tried to guess what this so called 'talent' involved. He was sure it had to involve cheating in some way.

'Come on, come on, tell me Marco,' he quickly replied.

'He can spin any number you want…'

Morris laughed. 'I'm sorry Marco. How many times have I heard that? It's not possible. You must know that?'

'Yes, let me explain. Not any number as I said. Sorry- but a section of the wheel. Sam, you remember the last investigation you did before quitting- Javonic-Tosa the Wheel Watcher?'

'Yes, of course- what are you saying?' However, he was starting to put the dots together.

'Well, if Javonic could figure out when and where the ball was going to drop from the spin, a dealer surely can as well.'

'Ah. You mean a section of the wheel? Yes, that's true. From using the speed of the wheel rotation and ball rotation you can guestimate where the ball will drop. For sure the ball does not drop straight into a number as we know, but if you have a good idea where it will drop you can bet in that section of the wheel around it and your chances of winning increase hugely. But that takes a very special skill and amazingly quick mental calculation.'

'Which Roberto has!' said Marco. 'Just like Javonic watching games for hundreds of hours, Roberto actually learnt from dealing.'

'How good is he actually? Lots of dealers brag about how they can spin any section, or number. Mostly rubbish.'

'Oh, he is very good Sam. He showed me, right here - he was that confident. He would tell me a number and then spin the ball. Eighty per cent of the time the ball landed within eight numbers each side of the number he had predicted. Amazing. This was over several days and about a thousand spins. It was not luck…'

'Eighty per cent,' exclaimed Morris, making some calculations in his head. 'That is incredible- what an advantage to anyone playing with him and he was trying to spin for them. Eighty…it should have been around twenty-five. I'm amazed. Are you really sure Marco?'

'Yes- amazing, like you said. He is an honest boy- he only wanted to learn to do this out of interest after we talked about Javonic, but he swears that he has never used it for his own profit, or anyone else's. He just spins normally, but he says he always calculates where the ball will drop to keep in practice, but just does not tell anyone. Now is the time, I am thinking.'

'Would he help?'

'I'm sure. The whole town is in angry about beautiful Maria. He will gladly help us get revenge.'

'Revenge, revenge,' thought Morris. 'How many millions has that killed.' But this time it sounded right…

'Ok,' he said coming back to the present. 'So this casino, it's one of these live games that is sent out on line right? So if he was spinning a section deliberately, how would anyone know. There are no actual players at these casinos are there?'

'Some have players and they just beam out the game and people can also bet on line in tune with the live game. Maria confirmed- this casino has live players also.'

'Ok. So how would it work exactly?' said Morris, trying to envisage the scene.

'The way I was thinking, at a fixed time, Roberto starts spinning so that the ball will land in the same general section as the winning number before. Say number twenty-six was the last number, so he spins to try and make the ball drop in the section around twenty-six. Our players will bet these sections and win. Easy!"

Morris frowned. 'So you will send a team there just to bet? There are table limits for each player. They will win, but it's not huge stuff…'

'No,' replied Marco quickly. 'We do not send a team. The players will be on line. From all over the world. Thousands of them. All betting the correct section…

'Don't understand. How will they know about Marco's spin?'

Marco laughed down the phone. 'We will tell them!'

'How the hell will you do that?'

'Roberto has been telling me. There is a thing called on line betting chat. Some of them are more or less hidden- nearly impossible to find. Roberto follows them, told me they are all asking the same question…'how can I win at roulette?' They talk about all the possibilities and probabilities and this includes cheating. If we spread the word quietly we can get thousands of people betting as Marco spins. If it all works out well, the casino will be ruined, no matter how much they make just now.'

'Ok, understand, but I'm sure most people would not believe such a golden opportunity to make money. They would be too skeptical to bet I reckon,' Morris said.

'So we tell them to watch a few spins and work it out for themselves. Once they see what Roberto is doing they will jump in and we have our revenge.'

'You don't want to make money out of this yourself? Sell the information about Roberto?'

'This time no. It is not about money. In fact, I will prevent anyone from Tolo to have a bet, in case it leads to suspicion. All the bettors are registered and could be traced if someone looked into it closely enough.'

'Ok. What about Marco though. Suspicion will fall on him alright?'

'I'm sure he will be willing to take the risk. He can shrug and just say he span the ball and the players thousands of miles away got lucky. If they ask about

Maria he can say they are both from Italy, but that's the only connection. He should be fine. At most they will probably just sack him. He will be fine with that too, I'm sure. What do you think about it all Sam?'

Morris could only laugh. 'You are as devious as ever Marco. What can I say. Its brilliant. If and when Anne Smith phones, I would just say you talked to me and tell her to just sit back and keep an eye on the news- because if it goes like you plan, this will be in the news for sure.'

Marco agreed. The conversation moved on to other topics and Marco ended by telling Morris that he would keep him updated after he confirmed Roberto's cooperation and as things progressed thereafter. Morris was glad that he would. He was feeling the old adrenalin pumping through him again trying to imagine the scene when Roberto dropped the ball into a fixed section spin after spin…

CHAPTER 19

Two days later Anne Smith got a call while having lunch with Liz Hislop.

'Is that Anne Smith?' said a smooth, but firm voice.

'Hello, yes, who is speaking?' She conveyed a quizzical look towards Liz.

'I am Johnny Cossar Head of Security at the casino you visited the other night. My boss has asked me to ask you why you followed him home the other night. Right up to his house.'

Anne was in shock. She had no idea how she had been recognised and then identified. She tried to bluster.

'I'm afraid I have no idea what you are talking about. Casino?' Liz, seeing her discomfort had leant forward, listening intently now. There was a sigh on the other end of the phone.

'Anne Smith, wife of deceased patron Ian Smith. We have your signature when you joined the club the other night. We have you on CCTV as well following my boss home…'

'I'm afraid that...'

'Just be quiet please Ms. Smith. I will tell you this once and once only. Leave Mr Liddle alone from now on. If you don't there will be serious consequences. Good bye.'

The line went dead. Anne stared into the distance.

'What is it,' said Liz eagerly. 'Bad news.'

Anne relayed the detail of the call.

'Bugger, he knows who you are. That could mean trouble if you try and rip him off the casino. Did you phone that Italian guy yet that Sam told you about?'

'No, Sam phoned back a couple of hours later and told me all was in hand and I did not need to do anything except watch the news for a scam story from Cyprus. I'm a bit confused, but no, I did not phone. What a bastard this Liddle is. Getting someone to threaten me. Even if somehow he did not know before Ian was my husband, he knows now. Oh, how I want him to get hurt. Now more than ever.'

'Phone Sam now and see what he says I think is a good idea,' said Liz, reaching over and squeezing Anne's hand.

Anne nodded called Morris, got through and explained the call she had just received.

'I guess he is worried that you might try and do something since you were mad enough to follow him all the way home,' Morris said. 'But don't worry. You will get your satisfaction and there will be no come back for you. I talked to Marco an hour ago. It's all in place for tomorrow night- staring at 01:00. I have been thinking that we should all meet up and enjoy the show together. Wasn't sure where, but just had an idea. You need to be in a place where you can be seen when it kicks off, so that you cannot be associated with the hit in any way. And what better place than where Frank Liddle will be- in his casino.

'You think? Anne said.

'Definitely. There will be loads of CCTV cameras there and we can sit calmly playing slot machines while Frank and his Turkish associates are being wiped out. Verifiable non –involvement. I'll get Marco to keep us updated as the whole thing unfolds. So we will all meet up at the casino around mid-night. Ok?'

Anne saw the merits in the location, but was a bit worried about going there after receiving threats to avoid Liddle. She conveyed her fears to Morris.

'You will be ok. It's too public for them to do anything and Stuart and I will be there too. They won't do anything there, for sure. See you all at midnight tomorrow. I remember there is a pub directly opposite the casino. See you in there?'

Anne hesitated, then agreed, ended the call and updated Liz. She looked nervous, but there was no mistaking the shared feeling of excitement between them. Neither had done anything like this before.

The on line Roulette chat site where the games tactics and tips were shared between a following of around five thousand Gambling addicts and those just curious about the game was called '37 Analysis'.' Its creator remained anonymous and it could not easily be found on line, being layered through other Gaming chat groups. Nevertheless, the followers were dedicated, educated and well resourced. Anecdotes were passed on and data analysis was frequently posted. Two days before Marco and Roberto had planned to enact the scam the following post appeared.

'Let's Play C (Cyprus) live casino (see link). Sunday morning at either 01:05. Or 01:25. Male dealer (belt with small dragon head) will be section spinning. 80% success rate for numbers 8 to either side of last winning number. Time periods 40 minutes, or until taken off table. Not convinced? Watch first 5 spins and make up your own mind. No need for good luck- you don't need it. Do not mention this outside this site. Reason for info is personal, but genuine and 100% morally deserved.'

The author was given as the Wizard and was posted by one of Roberto's friends from Milan who Roberto knew posted some good, reliable information on '37 Analysis,' so he had prior creditability. There were one or two comments soon after the post but it slowly mushroomed and by the time of a few hours before the scam was due to start it had increased to a flurry of excited comments and commitments. There was plenty of skepticism, but the lure of easy money and possibly plenty of it, allied to the trustworthiness of the author convinced many to commit to having a go. Roberto followed the posts eagerly and contacted Marco to inform him that he believed up to half of the members (two – three thousand) would at least place some bets. They both agreed that would be enough to cause huge financial damage to Liddle and his Turkish associates.

Morris received the message from Capone that all was in place just after midnight in the pub opposite the casino. Stuart, Liz and Anne arrived a few moments later and he bought a round while informing them of the news. They talked while having their drinks. There was no mistaking the building excitement. Even Morris, a Scam expert, felt the flow of adrenaline. They finished and crossed the road and entered the casino reception. There, as planned, Anne asked the Receptionist to call the security Manager and after she did so, Johnny Cossar arrived a few moments later, looking stern and authoritarian.

Anne smiled and presented her hand which Cossar accepted. She affected her best coy demeanor.

'Mr Cossar. Thank you for coming down. I am Anne Smith who you phoned. Please accept my apologies for what I did. My husband died recently and he used to come here and knew Frank. I had wanted to talk to him about Ian, but he left the casino. I thought maybe I could talk to him at his house about Ian, but when I got there I realised it was a stupid thing to do. We even passed the spot where Ian was run over… Please pass on my apologies to Mr Liddle. They found the person who ran Ian over by the way, so I hope Mr Liddle does not think I blamed him in any way. Please tell him.'

Cossar was looking directly in her eye as she spoke. He wasn't sure, but eventually concluded that since she had come in person she was probably telling the truth. Death affected people in funny ways. Nevertheless, he told Anne to wait and called Liddle.

'What did you think Johnny? Ok, to let her in? She won't come near me?' Liddle asked.

'Aye, should be ok, seems a harmless old lady, but I'll remind her not to.'

He moved back to Anne. Morris, and Liz and Stuart had finished registering and were standing at the Reception counter.

'Mrs Smith. I talked to Mr Liddle and he has accepted your apology and you and your friends may enter. However, he is a busy man who needs no distractions, so please do not approach him.'

Anne smiled. 'Thank you so much. Don't worry, my friends and I will just have a drink and play Slots. Tell Mr Liddle thanks please…'

She rejoined Morris and the Hislops and they entered the casino. Morris leant closer to her.

'Perfect. Your presence here will be remembered and there can be no suspicion that you were involved in what is coming up. Great. Ok, let's play Slots and wait for the messages…'

They ordered a drink from a waitress and gathered round a slot machine. Morris put fifty pounds in and Anne started playing. There was a ping on Morris's phone. He looked at the message.

'R. on break. Start 01:21.'

Inside the breakroom of the Let's Play casino Roberto sat looking as calm as possible. Was he up to the task? He felt ok, but he noticed a thin film of sweat on his palms. He immediately worried that this may affect his spins. He dried them on his trousers and looked around. Nearly time. 'here goes,' he said, getting to his feet. 'This is for you Maria…' He climbed the stairs to the casino and headed for the Roulette table. There were four players on the table. He wondered how many others were out there waiting…?

Inside his office in the Glasgow casino, Liddle was sipping a brandy. He admitted to himself that he had been worried about this Anne Smith following him. He had told Ian to keep their affair quiet as he knew from a previous liaison how the wife of a husband having an affair with another man could go down. Badly. But it looked like Ian had opened his mouth before being run over. 'Should have done it myself,' he smiled. Well it seemed fine now. If she had wanted to do anything she would hardly walk into his casino. He took another sip of his brandy and glanced at his computer screen. He received simultaneous data feeds from the main three on line casinos. Let's Play C (Cyprus), Let's Play R (Romania) and Let's Play M (Malta). He really could not believe how much money these places made. The received feeds were basic but sophisticated- passing on the profit made after every spin and total win for the Gaming day. Liddle loved watching the money rolling in. Of course sometimes the punters would get ahead for a while, but the law of large numbers always eventually sorted that out. It was 01:20. He decided on a walk around the casino. He was in a good mood and would pass that on to the Glasgow players he decided. He downed his drink and looked at the screen once more before leaving.

'Let's Play C. 01:21. $105. Total Gaming day: $3,050.'

Normal enough. That casino had made $105 profit on the last spin which occurred at 01:21 and $3,050 profit for the Gaming day so far. Very good. His share of the result was 25%. The winnings would be placed in his account by five in the morning exactly one hour after the end of the Gaming day and the same time requirement was also the deadline to cover any casino loss, but that had only happened a few times before for a few thousand dollars. His best day had been $368,000 profit for one day's work. He shook his head and left the office- still amazed at how much he was making.

At the Slot Machines, Morris's phone binged a message from Marco.

'Started. Following 37 Spins link. They have a live link to the game. R. now spinning.'

Morris passed on the message verbally, but discretely as the group carried on playing slots. Anne saw Frank Liddle leave his office, but he did not seem to recognize her as he moved around. Most of the players were Chinese and she could see Liddle was in a good mood as he nodded frequently to them and shook their hands. 'Bastard,' she thought. 'Please, please let this work.'

Morris's phone went again.

'First 3 all ok. In range. Comments on 37 saying they are going to go big now. R. looks calm.'

At 01:40. Liddle returned to his office. He phoned the bar and ordered another brandy. He looked at his screen again. Bit disappointing result for Lets Play Cyprus he noticed.

'Let's Play C. 01:39. -$22,074. Total Gaming day: -$31,010'

Looking at previous entries he noticed that the last three spins were all losers for the casino. This was fairly unusual as so many players playing normally meant all the numbers were equally covered, so a spin win was more or less guaranteed. His drink arrived. He now watched the screen with even more interest than usual. The next spin blinked up.

'Let's Play C. 01:43. -$240,770. Total Gaming day: -$271,780'

Liddle sat up erect and stared at the screen. He could only mutter 'what the fuck.'

Morris received a message at 01:46.

'Missed. First time. 37 estimated Casino down $240k +. Still good'

Liddle had been very relieved to see that after the message that the casino was down $271,780 the next spin had been better.

'Let's Play Cyprus. 01:45. +$45,000. Total Gaming day: -$226,780.'

'Phew.' The tide has turned, he smiled to himself chiding himself for his earlier feelings of panic.

The next message caused him to drop his drink.

'Let's Play Cyprus. 01:47 -$1,550,000. Total Gaming day: -$1,776,780.'

Liddle rose up kicked the desk chair against the wall and swore so loudly that within a minute Cossar came rushing through the door.

'Mr Liddle, Mr Liddle, what's the matter? I thought someone was in here. Are you ok?'

Liddle looked at him and remembered that his on line activities were strictly on a need to know bases. He thought quickly.

'Sorry Johnny. I just dropped my drink and got a bit angry. Expensive Brandy that…'

Meanwhile the next spin came up on the screen. This time Liddle did not see it.

'Let's Play Cyprus. 01:50. -$4,981,000. Total Gaming day: -$6,757,780.'

Morris and company had received a message to at 01:45 informing him that it was going well and the bets were now very big as everyone could see that the promised sections were hitting and even more than expected. Morris, Anne and the Hislops all turned when they heard the noise in the office. The Security manager then rushed in but left a few moments later looking somewhat bewildered. 'Ha,' Morris said. 'Sounds like Liddell has got angry about something. Wonder if he is following the same game we are?' He laughed and squeezed Anne's hand. She was beaming like a spoilt kitten lapping up milk.

In the office Liddle had just seen the previous spin data when the latest message flashed up.

'Let's Play Cyprus. 01:54. -$16,221,000. Total Gaming day: -$22,978,780.'

He locked the door and switched on the live feed of the game. He peered at the dealer and the patrons.

All looked normal. 'What the fuck is happening?' he muttered.

He remained motionless, realising he was now facing totally ruin. He tried to phone his Turkish contacts, but he knew it was only 5am in Istanbul and they would not even look at their phones till around eight am UK time. Liddle could only stare blankly at the screen. From 01:54 till 02:21 the results steadily worsened, with only two spins being a win for the casino. He looked at the screen. Result for the day was a scarcely believable loss of $34,888,000. He used the calculator on his phone to work out his share. $8,722,000. He knew someone must have cheated them, but could not figure how. It did not matter. The money would already be in the punters accounts and they would never get it back. He had less than three hours to raise and transfer 6.3 million pounds into the company account. He knew that was all he had and more, but if he didn't pay it he would not be around for much longer. He worked frantically, transferring, borrowing and begging for the money. At 04:50 he deposited the money. He was wiped out. Not just for now, but for as long as he could imagine. He had had to borrow 2 million pounds at an interest rate of 25%. Just after five fifteen he walked out of the office slowly, head bowed and headed for the exit.

Outside the office at the Slots Machines, Morris et al had decided to wait and see if there was any reaction when Liddle eventually left his office. Marco had sent him a last message that they reckoned the casino must have lost around $20 million. If Liddle knew how much he had lost, as they suspected he did, it would be a site for sore eyes. Anne especially did not want to leave until she had seen Liddle come out. That was what it had all been about, after all. They had not been disappointed. Liddle slowly emerged from his office. He looked ashen faced and completely subdued. Now that they had seen him and the casino was closing they found themselves only a few meters behind Liddle as he passed reception and left the casino. He walked slowly, his head not moving, just staring at some distant, fixed point. He started to cross the road. Morris saw the car coming and started to move towards Liddle. Anne grabbed his arm, her eyes on fire.

'No- wait! Let him…'

Morris hesitated and as he turned briefly to face Anne, there was a muffled thud and the sound of tires coming to a rapid halt. They watched as Liddle was hit by the car and in almost slow motion was tossed ten meters along the road. He hit the ground and lay motionless. The brief silence was ended by the sounds of Cossar and two Security guards rushing from the casino entrance, before they too came to a sudden halt. Liz covered her face with her hands, Stuart and Morris looked stunned. Morris glanced at Anne. She looked calm, almost serene.

She looked at him. 'Full circle Sam, full circle. Look at the time…five thirty.' She looked up at the sky. 'That's for you, you wee bastard.'

'Jesus, he's dead,' they heard Cossar shout.

Morris stood still for a minute on the pavement shaking his head. He just wanted to get home and try and forget about this. He had played a part in the death of a man he realised. Looking around at Stuart and Liz, he could see that the same thought was crossing their minds. What Anne was thinking, he could only guess. Morris ushered the group together and up Sauchiehall street before the ambulance, or police arrived. What he and they would say to them if it was necessary could wait for at least a few hours.

On wakening in the early afternoon after Liddle's death, Morris had phoned Frazer and explained that he had been at the scene and the background behind it and asking if the police would need statements. It took him nearly fifteen minutes to relate the whole story. Frazer had listened in silence and when Morris had finished said. 'Ok. Thanks for that Sam. I can see you guys are probably blaming yourself because what you organised led to his death. But, I can tell you that this Liddle guy was a bad one. Well known to us. Involved in many illegal activities and not just the on line Gaming business. He dabbled in drug trading for example. So believe me in the same way you feel responsible for taking actions that led to him being run over- he definitely killed people by his. And no, we won't need to interview you guys. There were other witnesses. It was a clear accident. End of story- but thanks for volunteering. I know how you think Sam. Forget it. Go and have a pint. Concentrate on the good folk around you. Margaret arrived from Greece yet?

Morris thought that Alisdair Frazer certainly fell into the category of 'good guys' he had mentioned. Gauging his guilt and trying to dissipate it. But there was something he had to say to finish this macabre Hit and Run case.

'Ok, thanks pal. Aye- arrived yesterday. There is one other thing I'm worried about and don't know if I should pursue- but I'll tell you. I saw the look on Anne's face – she was pleased by Liddle being killed- I could see it. Just made me start to think about William Ware and if it really was the accident she says it was…?'

'That one we will never know,' Frazer replied quickly. 'I too wondered- but save a confession we would never get a conviction. If she did do it, and once her feelings of what she thought was justified revenge start to lessen, she will have to live with that for the rest of her life. That's not as easy as most people think.'

'Well ok, but just thought I should tell you my suspicions. And I am about to take your advice and go for a pint. The relative tranquility of the Doublet. beckons!'

CHAPTER 20

It was six months later and Morris was in the pub having a pint, waiting for his kids and Linda to join him before heading out for a pizza. He was looking forward to that. He looked around the bar from his regular seat. It was early Friday and the pub was busy. In the alcove Stuart and Liz Hislop were sitting together holding hands. 'Nice to see all is forgiven,' he smiled. Alasdair Don, the previous owner of the pub, was standing at the bar with several of his golf pals and chatting to them and latest owners- Paul and Claire Butler. As always Don looked content and greeted the familiar pub faces of which there were plenty. Standing at the bar was Phil Burns and sitting next to him, Gary Scott. They seemed to be good friends these days. 'Good for Gary,' he thought. It was good to have a friend to meet in the pub regularly – even though Burns was a little-well very - eccentric. The Doublet door opened making the particular noise that it always did. Morris looked up expecting it to be his children and Linda, but it was an attractive older lady. She walked over to Gary and kissed him on the cheek. Gary smiled. His new girlfriend from the travel agency in Byres road Morris realised. Gary had mentioned her- Lorna Boyd. They looked good with each other. Remembering Julia Sinclair, Morris' thoughts drifted back to the Hit and Run just up the road from where he now sat. He shook his head. How many deaths had there been connected to it? Ian Smith obviously, but also, William Ware, Julia Sinclair, Frank Liddell and Ronald Burns- killed a few months ago in prison in much the same way as he had murdered Sinclair. All would be here today if not for that accident. 'And you can probably add Anne Smith to that list as well,' Morris concluded remembering what Frazer had said to him about postponed guilt. She had been found dead in her flat three weeks before. She had died by swallowing her own vomit. Morris remembered the night in her flat. No one to save her this time around. Dozens of empty gin bottles had been found strewn around her flat. The Lets Play scam had made the papers. An Investigation was in progress even though the casino was illegal. The Turkish mafia had called in the police- accepting any forthcoming fine in the hope they could retrieve the USD 35 million that had been lost. Six months later, enquiries were getting nowhere. 'Hadn't been enough for you Anne?' Morris thought, trying to dispel the image Anne's final hours from his mind. He was helped by the timely arrival of his son, daughter and Linda coming through he Doublet door, just as his own mother and father and countless lost friends had done in years gone by. Morris took it all in. He felt pangs of emotion. Too many were gone, but there were a lot of good people still around. He rose from his chair, gave his rather surprised children a lingering hug, put his arm round Linda' waist, kissed her and ushered them to his table and headed to the bar. Big John was there waiting for an order. Morris said hello, which was reciprocated, but he could see John was looking pensive. 'You ok pal?' he offered as John collected the drinks and tuned towards the tables. John hesitated, then looked around and sighed. 'Actually, not really. Got a wee problem. Bit sensitive. I wonder if you could maybe help me sort it out. You know Slight Jimmy the tobacco guy?'

'Aye, sure. What's up?' Morris said.

'He's got sixty quid of my cash and he has disappeared. Could you maybe make a few enquiries with your police pal or anyone else?'

'Give us a break pal,' Morris thought, but found himself replying. 'Sure John, I'll see what I can do,' not realising what was in store for him as a result of his words. But that's another tale…

ABOUT THE DOUBLET.

The Doublet on Park Road opened in 1962 and its Lounge bar upstairs in 1971. The Doublet was once described in The List as "probably Glasgow's finest pub," Previous licensee Alistair Don pointed out the quote to one of his regulars and the immediate response was to take out the word 'probably'. The Doublet was one of the first bars in Glasgow to sell real ale. One of the big attractions for many of the regulars (and for me too) is the pub looks more or less the same as it did fifty years ago. Mr Don once explained. "My customers don't want me to change it. Obviously it's been redecorated, but everything goes back in roughly the same place. The Doublet is quirky and popular so why change something that is not broken.' Alistair Don retired from the trade at the age of 69 and sold the pub in 2016 to new owners Paul and Claire Butler.

DAVID R.D. ROLLO

As can probably be gauged from the book, I am familiar with the Doublet and first visited in 1977, or as soon as I was eighteen. However, I cannot claim to be a regular having lived and worked abroad most of my life. The pubs I remember circa 1977 were The Doublet, Pewter Pot, Curlers, The Western and Tennents (which had only allowed women to enter after a 1971 protest. It wasn't until the 1940's that women were even allowed to serve behind bars in Glasgow I found when doing a bit of research. The Calvinistic reasoning being that female barmaids would only encourage the men to drink more —as if they were holding back).

From 1978 to 1982 I was a student at Stirling University but my parents had a flat in the West End so I visited fairly regularly and pubs were always on the agenda. After graduation I drifted into Casinos and left for South Africa – Sun City in 1983. Since than I have worked in Poland, Russia, Greece and presently Vietnam. On trips home the plan of attack was always the same. Dump the case, several hours in the Doublet and a Fish Supper from the Philadelphia. That's been the same routine for forty years nearly. As noted above, I appreciate the fact that the Doublet has changed so little since I first visited. Like the mountain Suilven, seeing it unchnaged brings comfort and warm recollections. Unfortunately, though the bar remains as was, the regulars have changed over the years and many will not ever be back for a pint and a chat. These include my mother and father, Elaine and David, and too many close friends to mention. By an amazing coincidence, I was fortunate enough to be able to buy a flat just next door to the pub (the tunnel connecting the two should be completed soon), so going out for a pint there involves a walk of only 12 meters there and (usually) a similar distance on the way back. Writing this now, I wish I was there, sitting in the warm pub chatting to the regulars, talking politics and discussing takes on the day's events with a large dollop of humour and glancing at the door to see which Glasgow character was going to pop in next…Cheers!

David Rollo. December 2021.
Phu Quoc. Vietnam.

Lightning Source UK Ltd.
Milton Keynes UK
UKHW010741060223
416537UK00003B/980